Cheaper to Keep Her

KS Publications
www.kikiswinson.net

Don't Miss Out On These Other Titles:

Wifey
I'm Still Wifey
Life After Wifey
Still Wifey Material
Wifey 4-Life

Mad Shambles
The Candy Shop
Still Candy Shopping
A Sticky Situation
Sleeping with the Enemy (with Wahida Clark)
Heist (with De'nesha Diamond)
Playing Dirty
Notorious

A STORY BY UNIQUE

PROLOGUE

"**B**itch! You better open this fucking door!"
When I heard his voice, the banging and then the kicking on the door, my heart sank into the pit of my stomach. A hot flash came over my body at the sound of his deep, baritone voice. I could tell he was more than livid. I immediately started rushing through the luxury high-rise condominium I had been living in for the past six months. Duke owned it. It was time to put my Plan B into motion. Quick, fast and in a hurry.

"Damn, damn, shit!" I cursed as I gathered shit up. I didn't know how I had let myself get caught slipping. I planned to be the fuck out of dodge before Duke could get wind of my bad deeds. I had definitely not planned my escape correctly.

"Lynise!" Duke's voice boomed again with additional angry urgency. He started banging even harder and jiggling the doorknob. I was scared too death, but I wasn't shocked. I knew sooner or later he would come. After all the shit I had done to him, I would've come after my ass too.

"Lynise! Open this fucking door now!" Duke continued to bark from the other side of the door. He didn't sound like the man I had met and fell in love with. He damn sure didn't sound like he was about to shower me with cash and gifts like he used to. Not after all the shit I had done . . . or un-done, I should say.

"Open the fucking door!" he screamed again.

I was shaking all over now. From the sound of his voice I could tell he wasn't fucking around.

"Shit!" I whispered as I slung my bag of money over my shoulder and thought about my escape. I whirled around aimlessly but soon realized that my Plan B didn't include Duke being at the front door of his fifth floor condo. There was nowhere for me to go. It was only one way in and one way out and I damn sure wasn't jumping off the balcony. If it was the second floor, maybe I would've taken a chance but I wasn't trying to die.

"Fuck! Fuck! Fuck!" I cursed as I saw my time running out. Duke was a six foot tall hunk of solid muscle. I knew I had no wins.

"Bitch! I'm about to take this fucking door down!" Duke screamed. This time I could hear him hitting the door hard. I couldn't tell if he was kicking the door or putting his shoulder into it. Although it was his condo, I had changed the locks to keep his ass out.

I spun around and around repeatedly, trying to get my thoughts together before the hinges gave in to his brute power. Hiding the money I had stolen was paramount. My mind kept beating that thought in my head. I raced into the master bedroom and rushed into the walk-in closet. I began frantically snatching clothes off the hangers. I needed to use them to hide my bag of cash.

Wham!

"Oh my God!" I blurted out when I heard the front door slam open with a clang. I threw the bag onto the floor and covered it with piles of designer clothes. Things Duke and I had shopped for together when shit was good between us.

"Bitch, you thought I was playing with you?" Duke's powerful voice roared. "Didn't I tell you, you had to get the fuck out of my crib?"

He was up on me within seconds. I stood defenseless as he advanced on me so fast I didn't even have time to react. I threw my hands up, trying to shield myself from what I expected to come when he reached out for me. But I was too late. He grabbed me around my neck so hard and tight I could swear little pieces of my esophagus had crumbled.

"Duke, wait!" I said in a raspy voice as he squeezed my neck harder. I started scratching at his big hands trying to free myself so I could breathe.

"What bitch? I told you if you ever fucked with me you wouldn't like it!" he snarled. Tears immediately rushed down my face as I fought for air. "Ain't no use in crying now. You should've thought 'bout that shit a long time ago."

Duke finally released me with a shove. I went stumbling back and fell on my ass so hard it started throbbing. I tried to scramble up off the floor, but before I could get my bearings I felt his hands on me again. His strong hand was winding into my long hair.

"Ouch!" I wailed, bending my head to try to relieve some of the pressure he was putting on my head.

Duke yanked me up by my hair. Sharp, stabbing pains shot through my scalp.

"Owww!" I cried out as he wrung me around by my hair. I tried to put my small hands on top of his huge, animal hands, but it was no use. Hands I had once loved, I now despised and wished would just fall off.

"You thought it was all good right! You a fucking trifling ass bitch and I want you the fuck out of here!" Duke gritted. Then he lifted his free hand and slapped me across my face with all his might.

"Pl-pl-pl-please!" I begged him for mercy. But Duke hit me again.

I was crying hysterically. Partly from the pain of his abuse, but more so from our past. I would have never thought our relationship would come to this. It had been a long road and all I wanted to do was teach him a lesson when I did the shit I did. I never thought I would have been facing this type of torment.

"I want all your shit out of here, you scandalous bitch! And don't take nothing that I fucking bought!" Duke roared, then he hit me again. This time I felt blood trickle from my nose. My ears were still ringing from the previous blow to my head. He hit me again. I was sure he had knocked one of my teeth loose.

"Yo Ak, get this bitch shit and throw it the fuck out," Duke called out to one of his boys. He never traveled anywhere alone. There were always two dudes with him at all times. The one I knew as Chris rushed into the closet and started scooping up my clothes and shoes.

"Wait!" I screamed, but it was for nothing.

"Shut the fuck up!" Duke screamed in response, slapping me again.

I could actually feel my eyes starting to swell. I finally gave up. My spirit was broken, my body was sore. I watched as Chris and another one of Duke's boys slid back the glass balcony doors and started tossing all my shit over. I doubled over crying. More and more shit went over and I was sure it was raining down on the beautifully manicured lawn below.

"Yeah . . . that's enough. Don't throw none of that jewelry or those furs outside. I got bitches I could give that shit to," Duke said maliciously. His words hurt. "A'ight bitch. . . ya time is up."

I shrunk back thinking he was going to hit me again. But he didn't. He grabbed me by the arm roughly. "Oww!" I cried out.

Duke was squeezing my arm so hard the pain was crazy. "Let's go," he said, pulling me towards the door.

"Nooooo!" I screamed and then I dropped my body weight down towards the floor so he couldn't pull me.

"Oh bitch, you getting the fuck outta here," Duke roared. He bent down, hoisted me over his shoulder and started carrying me kicking and screaming towards the door.

"You can't do this to me! You will regret this Duke Carrington!!" I hollered.

"Fuck you!" he spat in return, opening the condo door and tossing me out into the hallway like a piece of discarded trash. I can't even describe the feeling that came over me. It was a mixture of hurt, shame and embarrassment all rolled into one.

Duke slammed the door in my face and I yelled for him to listen to me. My cries fell on deaf ears. My shoulders slumped down in defeat. Duke had left me in the hallway with no shoes, a short nightgown and nothing but my belongings on the lawn outside. I didn't even have the key to my BMW X6.

"Aggghhh!" I grunted in anger and frustration as I raked my hands through my tangled hair. I vowed from that minute on that Duke Carrington would learn just what all men have been saying for years . . . *it's cheaper to keep her.*

As I limped down the hallway of the building, all of the memories of how I had gotten to this point came rushing back.

CHAPTER 1

MAGIC CITY

*O*ne *Year Earlier.*
 I walked into the *Magic City* and was immediately disgusted by the crowd that was already hanging around my post.

Same shit, different day, I thought to myself. I had been working at the well known strip club for a minute and it seemed like each passing month, more and more thirsty ass niggas showed up to spend their hard earned money on a fantasy. I crinkled my face and looked at my watch just to make sure I had the right time. It was only eight-thirty in the evening and niggas were already starting to pack the club. I mean, damn, didn't they have wives at home giving them some ass. Maybe not, judging from how they came up in the *club* and made it rain almost every night.

I noticed a few of the regulars sitting around. Of course, the ones that were there early were the older, more broke niggas that wanted to take advantage of the specials. The ballers usually rolled in after midnight and when they did all the girls who worked at the *club* would put their best foot forward and try to get some of that baller dough.

I scanned the bar area and rolled my eyes as I headed for my post behind the bar. I wasn't no stripper chick. Bartending was my thing. I could mix the fuck out of a drink, but I wasn't about to shake my ass for dollars. I didn't know how the chicks up in the *Magic City* did it. Men touching them all over their bodies for as little as a single dollar bill. Hell naw! Not me. All of those different hands all over my body, I would be sick after that shit. Then all that ass shaking, pole hopping and these chicks may or may not make a single dime. Not me, I needed guaranteed money. Even though these thirsty ass dudes didn't tip bartenders like they used to, they still wanted to sit up in my face and try to spit game my way. I probably turned down sixty niggas a night. I had so many of them telling me how beautiful I was. Yeah, yeah, I've heard it all. One nigga even told me I looked like Jada Pinkett Smith. Well, a few people told me that. Maybe it's true, maybe not. I did know that I was official. I kept my shit together: hair, nails and clothes. Although money was definitely an issue, the package had to be presentable.

As a bartender, I had listened to every type of story about life there was, especially the same old story men told about their dry ass wives at home who didn't give up the pussy. Yada, yada, yada. All that said, bartending at the *club* paid the bills. At least until a better opportunity came along, bartending was my gig.

I switched my ass past the early bird hounds who were already surrounding the bar trying to be the first to get their seats at the stage. It was Thursday, which meant, their favorite stripper was about to grace them with her presence.

Diamond was all the rage at the *Magic City* and she was also my best friend and roommate. She had left for work before I did since she had to set up her look and her music. She was the club's Thursday night feature. A different stripper was featured each night of the week.

Needless to say, Thursdays were when the club was most packed. All the men loved Diamond. I mean, she was beautiful. She had a sweet baby face and the body of a video vixen.

I was almost to my post behind the bar when I felt a presence. I jumped.

"It's about damn time you showed the hell up!" I heard the voice and then felt somebody grab my arm.

"What the—" My statement was cut off. I was a bit thrown off.

"Lynise . . . I need a big favor," Diamond said in a pleading voice. Her words rushed out of her mouth like running water. She looked as if she had seen a damn ghost.

"Damn girl, you scared me grabbing on me like that," I huffed, looking at Diamond as if she was crazy. "What's the matter with you?" I asked confused.

"I need to borrow some cash quick before Neeko gets here. I ain't got the money to pay for my sets tonight," Diamond said, with urgency in her voice. She was rubbing her arms fanatically. The nervousness was written all over her face. I hated when she acted spooked and it had been happening more often lately. I sucked my teeth at her.

"Why you need to borrow money Diamond? Didn't you do a couple of sets last night? I saw niggas making it rain all around you," I said, frustrated. There was no reason Diamond didn't have any money when I was sure she had probably made over five hundred dollars just the night before.

"I know but I had to loan some to Brian," Diamond replied.

I threw my hands up in her face. I already knew she had given her no-good ass, wanna-be hustler boyfriend her money. I despised Diamond's boyfriend, Brian, but I tried to stay out of her business. He looked and acted like a buster if you asked me. However, Diamond was madly in love with his raggedy ass. He always had his hand out. I told her a million times it was supposed to be the other way around. Brian should've been taking care of her and trying to get her the hell up out of the *Magic City*. That's the way I saw it anyway. But there was no turning Diamond against the slouch.

"How the fuck you keep giving that nigga all your money?" I barked at her. "He is a grown ass, able bodied man! If he can't hustle up money or go get a damn job then you need to leave his ass! You a sucka for love or what?" I was fed up with Brian or better yet, I was fed up with Diamond falling for his shit. He was always at our apartment, eating up our food and never lifting a finger or putting a dime in the pot.

Diamond put her head down and wore a sad frown when I told her about herself and her man. I knew I had hurt her feelings and I was immediately sorry. I loved Diamond. She was my road dog. We had been through hell and back together. Neither one of us came from good homes and we had been down for each other for years. I just wanted her to make better decisions and be smarter with her money. I guess I should have been a little more sensitive. But I was too mad to be nice.

"Lynise, I wouldn't ask you if I didn't really need this," Diamond said somberly, shifting her weight from one foot to the other as if she had ants in her damn pants. I noticed she was fidgety as hell.

"Yo, this is the last time I'm loaning you money Diamond. We both struggling to pay rent and bills, remember?" I chastised her, taking my bag off my shoulder and placing it on a barstool so I could get my wallet. I dug into my purse and handed her a hundred dollars. That was enough for her to pay Neeko so she could do a few sets and make some money. That would lead to more sets. I knew she hated doing lap dances, but I was sure she would be doing some tonight to get some extra money. It was part of the *game*. And as much as we hated it, sometimes the *game* ruled us.

Diamond smiled and snatched the money from my hand. Then she threw her arms around my neck and hugged me. "Thanks girl, you're a lifesaver, that's why I love you," Diamond said, all of a sudden in a cheery mood.

"Just go knock them dead tonight bitch, 'cause we need to eat dammit," I said jokingly. Diamond smiled. She was so pretty when she smiled. I smiled back. I really loved my best friend. I watched as she trotted off to go get dressed for her sets. I shook my head as she finally disappeared down the steps to the Magic City's dressing rooms.

"That damn girl gon' drive my ass crazy," I mumbled.

I still didn't see how she thought this stripping shit was the best thing. The strippers at the *club* had to give Neeko, the club owner, twenty dollars for each set just to let them dance in his club. Then they had to pay the DJ twenty-five dollars for each set to play their theme music. Diamond told me on a good night she usually picked up around two hundred each set. To her, that made it worth it.

I couldn't help but think about the bad nights. To me, none of it was worth it. The idea of having hundreds, maybe thousands of strange hands all over my body freaked me out.

It didn't seem to really bother Diamond. However, deep down inside I think she felt just like I did about stripping.

One night, I watched from behind the bar as Diamond did her set. She got on her back at the edge of the stage, opened her legs like a scissor and spread her pussy lips open for a bunch of dudes sitting in the front row. I think she was just expecting them to throw dollars at her like usual. But I watched in horror as an old ass man, who I knew had no teeth, got up and actually put his mouth right on Diamond's spread eagle pussy and started slurping on her flesh. She definitely wasn't expecting it. The shock on her face spoke volumes. Diamond slammed her legs closed, smashing the man's head and he immediately jumped up. The man was smiling and wiping his lips. I thought I would throw up. Diamond looked horrified as she scrambled to her feet. The crowd of men burst into cheers and money flew everywhere. Although I could tell Diamond was disgusted, she stayed up there and picked up every dollar.

That night, as we drove to our apartment, neither one of us said a word about the incident. Once we got inside, I heard Diamond crying in the bathroom as she took a scalding hot shower. That's when I knew I would never, ever, strip for anyone.

I was four hours into my shift and I still had only made sixty dollars in tips. Talk about a slow ass night. I looked at the little chump change and sucked my teeth. Then just when I thought my night couldn't get any worse, in walks Devin, my sorry ass ex. I acted like I didn't see his ass at first, but he wasn't hard to miss.

"Wassup, Nini? You ready to take me back?" Devin said with a big smile on his face as he slid onto a barstool where I was mixing a drink for another one of the Magic City's regulars. I sucked my teeth and rolled my eyes at him. I slid the drink to my customer and rolled my eyes at the one dollar tip the cheap son-of-a-bitch placed on the bar. Devin noticed my disgust at the measly tip and of course he couldn't leave well enough alone.

"See if you was still with a nigga like me you wouldn't have to accept those penny ass tips," Devin said, flashing his perfect smile. Although I couldn't stand his ass for what he had done to me, he was still fine as hell.

"If you could keep your dick in your pants, maybe I would still be with you," I retorted, folding my arms across my chest.

"C'mon baby, you met me in a fucking strip club . . . did you really think I could control that," Devin said snidely. I swear I could've slapped the living shit out of him. All my thoughts of finding him fucking one of the white strippers in the club's champagne room came flooding back. The nerve of that muthafucka! While I was right outside at the bar working, he was fucking this bitch.

One of the other girls had come and told me I needed to go into the back and check things out. Initially, I was hesitant, but she insisted. When I found Devin and that bitch, I went off. I hit him in the head with a Heineken bottle and I tried to rip that bitch's hair extensions from her scalp. Neeko almost tossed my ass out in the street over that shit. My forgiveness was paying for a couple of broken mirrors and tables. From that day forward, I vowed never to fuck with none of the club's patrons. Devin had taught me a valuable lesson. If a nigga is in a strip club, he ain't gon' be faithful for shit.

"You're a fucking animal. Get the fuck out of my face," I spat in response to his snide comment. I turned my back to him and went about my work.

"A'ight, suit yourself. When you ready to get out the hood, holla at ya boy," he said. Then he slammed a fifty-dollar bill on the bar. As bad as I needed that fucking money, my pride wouldn't let me take it. I snatched it up, crumpled it into a ball and threw it at him.

"Don't ever leave no money on this fucking bar unless you're buying a drink!" I screamed in a pissed off state over the music. "I don't need or want shit you got, you fucking pencil dick asshole!" That asshole just laughed. But I was seething inside.

My anger was overcome by the sound of Diamond's theme music. I immediately forgot about that fucking idiot, Devin, and turned to see my girl do her thing.

Diamond looked stunning in her all-white corset and thong set. She had feathers in her hair and her make-up made her look like an angel. I watched her jump up on that pole with the skill of a gymnast. She twirled around it, letting her long, dancer's legs sway through the air artistically. Once she slid down to the floor, Diamond did a full split and with one pull of a trick string her corset flew off. The men in the crowd went crazy when Diamond's perfect C cup breasts flew free. She lifted one of her perky breasts and stuck her long tongue out and licked her own nipple. That was it. More cheers erupted from the crowd and once again, more money flew.

I couldn't front, the woman was damn good at what she did. She knew how to work her body and work the crowd. She continued her dance until she was completely naked. Then out the corner of my eye, I saw Brian walk into the club.

"Shit!" I grumbled.

Brian never came to the club. He knew what Diamond did for a living and had agreed to stay away. I was instantly on high alert when I saw him. He was looking around with a crazed look in his eyes.

"Awww shit," I whispered to myself. I saw Brian walking towards the stage. I started to make my way from behind the bar. Diamond was making her booty clap and a few of her regulars were slapping her butt cheeks and putting money in her ass crack.

Before I could make it to Brian's location or the stage, he had rushed to the edge of the stage. He grabbed one of the customers that had his hands on Diamond's ass and punched the man in his face. Screams erupted and the DJ started yelling on the microphone for security.

"Brian!" Diamond screeched when she noticed what was going on.

The crazy muthafucka was outnumbered. All the guys in the front were together. Brian had just punched their boy. It was only a matter of seconds before the entire group jumped him. They had him on the floor punching and kicking him. Bottles were flying, chairs were being turned over. Then other niggas in the club just started going in on each other. Sheer pandemonium broke out. What the fuck? Did they think this was a John Wayne fucking western or what?

The security guards were truly overwhelmed and they couldn't get a handle on all of the chaos. It wasn't until the DJ screamed that the police were on their way that everybody started to scatter. When the raucous group of guys jetted from the *club,* Brian was left in a bloody heap on the floor.

"Get him the fuck out of here!" Neeko screamed. Security came to hoist Brian's battered body off the floor.

Diamond ran to his side. "Brian! Please wake up!" she cried out. She grabbed his battered head and his bloody skull covered her breasts. It looked like something straight out of a horror movie.

"This your man? Well you can get the fuck outta here with him," Neeko boomed at Diamond. Security put both Diamond and Brian out. I rushed downstairs and grabbed Diamond's bag with her clothes. When I got outside I helped her get dressed. When the ambulance got there, they put Brian in the back and Diamond climbed in with him. I watched as it pulled off. I covered my eyes with my hands. I had to get my thoughts together.

Finally, I turned towards the club and stared at the glowing sign that was in the shape of a stiletto heel. I shook my head, knowing I had to go back inside to get my things and my money. It was like my feet were cemented to the ground. That was how much I didn't want to go back into the club. I was so tired of working there. The whole club scene was taking its toll on me physically and emotionally. I stood outside as if I was standing at the gates of hell, waiting for the Devil to eat me alive.

The building I stood outside, looking at with disdain, was the hell I wanted to escape. It was my albatross. There was always something and I was growing very weary of the entire scene. It took some time to get my feet to move, but I was able to walk through the club doors to collect my stuff. I walked slowly and deliberately as I headed back towards the bar. I could see the trail of Brian's blood from the stage leading to the exit doors. Neeko was clapping his hands and having people clean up the mess.

"It's back to business up in here! One dead monkey don't stop the show! We got ass to shake and pussy to show!" Neeko was calling out as he rallied the other strippers and his little crew to get the club back up and running.

I was disgusted with the whole scene. I was amazed at Neeko's lack of remorse or compassion. I rolled my eyes and bent down behind the bar to retrieve my money. It was my secret stash. Money I skimmed from the drinks I sold all night. That was the only way I could survive these days. I hurriedly stashed the money in my shoe and stood up.

I watched Neeko in disgust. He was acting like nothing had happened. "And tell your friend she is fired!" Neeko yelled at me.

"Oh please, Neeko . . . without Diamond's ass, this fucking club ain't gon' bring in no money, so I don't know who you fronting for," I spat back at his greasy ass.

Neeko paused and thought to himself. He knew I was absolutely right. There wasn't no way he was going to take a chance and let Diamond go work at one of the other competing clubs in the Tidewater area.

"Yeah, I thought that would shut you up. You will see Diamond's ass right up in here tomorrow night, so stop the yip yapping," I said sarcastically.

Neeko started yelling at the other girls. He knew better than to say anything else to me. I gathered my shit.

"I have to find a way to get the fuck out of this shit," I told myself.

I meant every word too.

I needed a way out and it had to be sooner . . . than later.

CHAPTER 2

EXCUSE ME MISS

The next night, I showed up to work dragging my feet. My body language and attitude showed that I didn't want to be at the *Magic City* and to top it off, I was tired as hell because of all the drama from the night before. Plus, Diamond came home early that morning from the hospital and kept me up most of the morning talking about what had happened to Brian. I tried to be nice but I had to finally let Diamond know that I couldn't give a fuck less what happened to Brian's no-good ass. Sometimes I couldn't understand why she loved that slouch, but I guess love is blind and evidently, stupid.

Diamond and I arrived at the club together. We had ridden in her little hoopty, a beat up Honda Civic. My car was once again in the damn shop. I was glad Diamond had decided to go back to the *club* after how Neeko had screamed at her. She needed to speak to Neeko to straighten out their little rift and I wanted to get an early start before any of the other bartenders got the jump on the first paying and tipping customers, so we came in together.

"Good luck talking to that ignorant nigga," I said to Diamond prior to us going in separate directions once we were inside the club.

"I know, right. I just gotta suck it up, Nini," Diamond commented. "Shit, we need the money. The landlord will be knocking on the first and you know ain't no grace period with his ass." She was right. I shook my head in agreement.

"Gimme a hug, girl, I need it," Diamond said to me as we stopped near a table at the midway point between Neeko's office and the bar. I smiled and hugged her for moral support.

"Be strong and stand your ground. He needs you just as much as you need him," I championed, giving Diamond a pep talk.

When we let go of each other, I went to walk away when I suddenly felt the heat of someone's touch on my arm. At first, I thought it was Diamond, but when I spun my head around I noticed it was a man grabbing me. There was a group of them sitting at one of the so-called *baller* tables. I curled my face into the nastiest frown. I didn't play any of those strip club muthfuckas touching me. I wasn't a fucking stripper and I intended on making that shit crystal clear.

"Get off me!" I barked, snatching my arm away without really even looking at the man. "Keep ya hands to yourself! I'm not one of these working girls up in here," I growled and started walking away.

"Damn, you are so beautiful, even with that frown on your face," the man said in a smooth baritone that was enough to make my insides feel mushy. His voice made me look at his face. *He was fine.* I could feel my face getting hot and knew I was starting to blush.

"Look, I'm not interested. I don't strip and I don't fuck with strip club dudes," I said dismissively. The man laughed like I had told him a real funny joke. That just disgusted me more. I still couldn't help but notice the one dimple in his left cheek and how masculine and sexy his face was. He immediately put me in the mind of Boris Kodjoe, the actor. I quickly shook off the feeling I was getting about the fine stranger and stalked off towards the bar before he could make me blush anymore.

"You can't go that far, Beautiful. I'll be here all night and I'm not giving up," he called after me. I secretly smiled but wouldn't dare let him see it. He had called me Beautiful. *Cute pick up line,* I thought to myself.

After about an hour behind the bar, I noticed that the club started getting real packed. It was Friday and all the hungry patrons had gotten paid and were ready to play. That worked for me. I just prayed they were drinking as much as they were buying a feel and lap dance. I was hoping and praying for a good night of tips. Like Diamond had reminded me, there were bills waiting for my ass at home.

Diamond had made up with Neeko and she was about to headline, even though it was Friday and it wasn't her night. Neeko was a scumbag, but he was a businessman. He had given her the stage, which was a smart business move. He knew who his moneymaker was up in the *club.* That's why I didn't know why he was fronting the night before. I shook my head and laughed internally. Only a fool or dumb businessman would fire a moneymaker such as Diamond.

I was mixing two Incredible Hulks for a husband and wife duo that always came to the *club* to spice up their sex life when Diamond came behind the bar. She was smiling and her face looked kind of weird. I gave her a weird expression in return, because she hardly ever came behind the bar and invaded my workspace.

"Don't you need to go get ready?" I asked her.

"Girl, I got time. Mix me up something sweet, but heavy," Diamond demanded, her voice lazy and heavy. If I didn't know any better I would've thought she was high or some shit. As soon as the thought came into my mind, I quickly dismissed it. I knew better. Diamond and I had made a pact a long time ago . . . drug free always.

I passed the husband and wife their mixture of Hennessy and Hpnotiq, and as I pulled my hand away, somebody touched it. I sucked my teeth when I saw that it was the same guy from earlier.

"Your skin is so soft," he said, once again flashing his one dimpled smile.

"You wouldn't know that if you would stop touching me. I told you earlier I don't like to be touched and I ain't interested in the game you're selling," I said flatly. Then I turned around so I could mix Diamond's drink. I brushed off my feeling about her possibly being high and chalked up her behavior to being tired from her hospital stay with Brian all night. I knew she probably needed the drink to ease her nerves and get herself mentally prepared for her set.

The stranger stayed there, as if he was waiting patiently for me to finish Diamond's drink. I had to admit, he was persistent. Most niggas would have already called me a stuck up bitch and left me alone by now.

"Girl, that nigga that is trying holler at you is fine as hell," Diamond commented, laughing afterwards. She made it very obvious that she was talking about him too.

"I don't care if he fine or not. He is up in a strip club looking for some quick ass," I replied. I made Diamond a

Pink Lady with an extra shot of Jamaican 151 rum and passed it to her.

"Lynise, if he was looking for ass he sure wouldn't be sitting at the damn bar trying to talk to the bartender," Diamond retorted. "Plus, that nigga is definitely caking off. I'm sure you can see that from here." I heard the seriousness in Diamond's tone and saw it on her face. I thought about that statement and she was right. I looked back at the guy and he was staring straight at me, which brought back that hot feeling inside my stomach and chest. Diamond took her drink to the head so fast I was shocked. She was definitely acting a little different than her normal self.

"Anyway, if he was just looking for ass he would be after me . . . the one who shakes her naked ass shamelessly every night, not you, the goody two shoes who refuses to take her clothes off bartender," Diamond said sternly. "Now you better let that nigga holler at you before you find me fucking him and collecting all his paper." Then she turned and walked away. Her words had hit me like a ton of bricks. She had definitely put shit into perspective for me.

"Ok, your bodyguard is gone now, can I order a drink?" the man called to me. It was clear he was not the type to give up. Either that or he really thought I was *Beautiful* and he just wanted to get to know me. Reluctantly, I went over to him.

"What can I get you," I asked, arms folded and head cocked to the side. I was still displaying my attitude, because it had become so routine for me. It was a defense mechanism I had acquired over the years. I felt like I had to protect my feelings at all times. I wasn't down for no bullshit from none of these cats in Virginia. Between my fucked up childhood and all the fucked up cats I had been with over the years, I was not up for the dumb shit anymore.

"You can get me your number and a date . . . tomorrow," the man answered. I rolled my eyes again.

"No, what kind of *drink* do you want?" I hissed. This time he didn't press, he just started talking.

"Trust me, baby girl, I ain't your average cat," he responded immediately. "I see you got much attitude and I'm digging that. I'm glad to know you don't let these dirty strip club niggas hit on you just for tips. Believe me, I don't pick up chicks in strip clubs either. I don't even frequent these jive ass places. I'm only here for my worker's birthday. The young cats that work for me chose this place. You know how it is when you young and horny. Well, maybe you being a woman you don't know. But in any case, the young dudes chose this place. I can assure you this is the first and last time you will see me in here. I'm a businessman. I damn sure don't have to buy lap dances and fantasy pussy."

His tone was very serious and his attack direct. For some reason, something about the way he spoke struck me as sincere. A slight chill came over me. I believed every word that came out of his mouth and I liked what he was saying. Everything he had said impressed me. I softened my attitude a bit and I found myself involuntarily smiling. I felt kind of dreamy. I heard Diamond's voice playing in my ear as well. Everything she had said was true . . . if this man wanted quick ass, he wouldn't be pursuing me. Not to mention looking at this fine ass man, with his flawless, smooth caramel skin and neatly trimmed beard was making me want to get to know him better. I guess the huge diamond studs and iced out pinky ring also helped to sway my attitude.

He noticed me sizing him up. "I can see your brain working," he smoothly stated. "It ain't much to think about, Beautiful. I'm not the last two bit nigga that hurt your feelings. I am a man. All I'm asking for is a chance to show you what I'm about."

I swallowed hard. That mushy feeling was definitely creeping back up on me. I was so digging the fact that he kept calling me Beautiful. I thought that was so respectful and gentleman-like. But I can't front. No matter how smooth and fine this stranger was, I was nervous to throw my hat back into the dating ring. I had been hurt one too many times.

"I'm Duke Carrington," the stranger introduced himself. "Since you seem to need a full background check, here is my card. Look me up on the internet and you will see just what I do." He paused with a quiet confidence. And he knew it. "Then give me a call so we can do something tomorrow. You don't look like you need a man, but I damn sure wanna show you what a real man can do . . . Beautiful."

Then he stood up from the bar. He placed two fresh and crisp one hundred dollar bills down and looked me directly in my eyes. "Make sure you call me. Um . . . I didn't get your name," he said quizzically. His eye contact was causing me to have hot flashes.

"Lynise," I said, almost whispering. Shit, for a few seconds, I forgot my own name. I was so in awe of how smooth this cat was.

"I think I will keep calling you Beautiful, it fits you so much better than Lynise," Duke the stranger said. And with that, he walked away from the bar.

And I watched every step he took.

CHAPTER 3

SUGAR DADDY

"Lynise Aaliyah Washington would you just pick up your damn cell phone and call the man already!" Diamond yelled at me.

We had just finished looking Duke up on the web. He had been right when he told me about himself. He was a well-known businessman in the Virginia Beach area. You name it, he was into it: real estate, landscaping, a few car washes, a couple of barbershops and beauty salons. Duke was a real entrepreneur. I read up on all his business ventures, but for some reason his style and swagger still made me feel that he was into something illegal. It was just a gut feeling I had.

"Give me that damn number then. I'll make a date with the nigga while Brian ass is laid up in the hospital useless as shit with broken ribs," Diamond said jokingly. At least, I think she was joking.

"Ok . . . ok . . . I'm gonna call him. He wanted to see me today and whatever we do has to be early before I gotta be at the *club* for work," I told Diamond.

"Girl, fuck the club and Neeko! You 'bout to become the wife of a rich man and get us both up outta this hood," Diamond sang, laughing afterwards. She seemed in much better spirits and more like herself than she had been in a while. I guess that was because that bum ass Brian was out of her life for a minute.

After a few more minutes of going back and forth with Diamond, I finally picked up the phone and called Duke's number. When his sexy voice filtered through the phone I closed my eyes. Diamond was making all kinds of faces. I could feel her presence.

Duke and I spoke for a few minutes and he agreed to pick me up. I gave him the address of the Marriott that was a few miles away from my apartment. I wasn't ready to let his ass know where I lived just yet. Duke said he would pick me up at five o'clock. That only left me an hour and a half to get ready. When I was sure he was off the phone I turned to Diamond with a panicked look on my face.

"Ok Miss Bitch, I took your advice and called him, but now the nigga will be here in an hour. What the fuck am I gonna put on and do with my hair!" I yelled at my best friend. "That is not enough time to get something done and find something at the mall to wear."

"Girl, please. You know you got Indian in your family," Diamond joked, putting her hand up against her mouth mocking an Indian call. We both busted out laughing. But my expression turned serious. I wasn't one to panic, but I felt some mild anxiety coming on.

"Seriously Diamond, what am I gonna do with my hair and what will I wear with a man like that," I said, getting back to the issue at hand. "Not like he is one of these regular slouches from around here."

"Lynise, your hair is long and beautiful, put some water and gel in that shit and wear it curly," Diamond told me, her voice of reassurance. "See, now look at my shit, this is gotta-have-a-perm hair." She playfully patted her hair. "Not you. You got that curly girl shit and besides, I love when you take your hair down out of that ratty ass ponytail you wear all the time."

I looked in the mirror at my reflection. Maybe Diamond was right. A little water, some gel, some make up and one of her hot outfits and I'd be set for my date with the businessman.

It took me close to an hour to get ready. I chose a black, fitted pencil skirt, a white collared shirt, which I left unbuttoned all the way down to my cleavage, and a threw on a pair of red pumps. Not too dress down and not too dress up.

"How does this look?" I asked Diamond as I tugged at my skirt.

"Nini, you look so gorgeous. I haven't seen you dressed up in a minute," Diamond said, faking like she was wiping tears of joy from her eyes. Her ass was hilarious and I enjoyed when we got a chance to spend time together like this.

"Your ass is silly!" I exclaimed, laughing at her. Diamond had hooked up my make-up. The fire red lipstick was taking some getting used to. I usually wore tans and browns on my lips, because my complexion was a bit light for the red stuff. Diamond had succeeded once again in convincing me that the red lipstick was the right touch for my outfit. I took her advice, of course. If there was anybody I trusted with fashion sense, it was Diamond.

I paced the sidewalk outside the Marriot waiting on Duke. I hated that I was there before him. I wondered if that would make me look thirsty or desperate in his eye. Usually the man had to wait on the woman, but being that Duke was such a classy businessman, I didn't want to have him waiting.

I stopped walking for a minute because my feet were already killing me in the pumps Diamond had loaned me. *Cheap shoes were a bitch to wear.* Just as I folded my arms impatiently and shifted my body weight from one foot to the other, I noticed a beautiful sleek, silver Porsche 911 pulling into the hotel's driveway. My heart started hammering in my chest like a bass drum. The windows were darkly tinted so I wasn't even sure it was Duke, but my gut told me that it was him. Sure enough, he slowly rolled down the passenger side window and leaned down so he could see me. He was flashing that sexy ass smile again.

"Hey Beautiful, you ready to go?" Duke sang out. I smiled back. I had told myself I would let my guard all the way down with Duke. I wanted to give him a chance. I wanted to give myself a chance to be treated like a woman should be treated by a real man.

I climbed into the car and I immediately recognized the scent of my favorite men's cologne—Platinum Chanel. I knew right then and there that if Duke played his cards right, he could have me, in every sense of the word.

"Beautiful you look so gorgeous tonight," Duke complimented me. I smiled and thanked him. "I have something real special planned for you. I know you work hard as hell at that little club, so a woman that works that hard also deserves to relax and play just as hard."

I was quiet. Sitting next to a man who was nothing but a gentleman, smelling good, in a hot ass whip and looking like real money. I was in heaven. I just needed a minute to take it all in.

Little old me, a girl from the hood that had been treated like shit since she was a kid. My mother and father were fucked up and I had knocked around Virginia living with various family members. I used to run away all the time and I thought hustling, street niggas were gonna save me from my life on the streets. I was wrong.

When I met Diamond, she was going through the same shit. We instantly hit it off and got an apartment together. She put me on to the *Magic City* and Neeko had tried to get me to strip. I just couldn't do that shit. So I started mixing drinks and became a full-time bartender.

Duke's car rode smoothly down the streets. I couldn't feel the bumps on the road. That told me the car was straight luxury. Duke was playing nice, easy going music and he was talking up a storm. I answered him if he asked me a question, but I didn't make much conversation. I was just taking it all in.

When we pulled up to the Virginia Beach Elegance Spa my mouth dropped open. This place was one of the top, high-class spas in our area and mostly rich people and celebrities frequented it.

"Oh my goodness. I can't let you take me here, Duke," I gasped. I knew the place costs at least a stack for just a massage. I looked over at him with my eyes stretched wide.

"Nonsense," he replied. "The entire staff inside knows me. They're expecting you, Beautiful. Don't worry, when you get inside they will take your clothes and hang them up. I selected the super deluxe package for you and it includes everything they offer. And that is only the beginning of our day, baby."

I smiled.

"I told you when fuck with me and you would see what it was all about," he said as he climbed out of his car.

I started getting out, but he knocked on the window and put his hand up telling me to stop. I was confused and I shrunk back down into the seat looking at him like he was crazy. That's when I saw him coming around to my side of the car. He opened the door for me and stretched out his hand for me to take so he could help me get out.

"A real man opens doors for his woman," Duke said smoothly. I was screaming inside of my head. I swear Duke could've had my pussy right then and there with that shit.

When I emerged from the spa I felt like a new woman. The massage was relaxing and my face felt silky and smooth from the sugar scrub facial I had received. Duke was waiting front and center for me.

"You look gorgeous as ever, baby." he complimented, extending his arms for a hug. I walked up to him, embraced and squeezed him tightly. *I was had.* At that moment, I could've stayed in his arms all day and night.

"Thank you for everything. It was so nice and relaxing. I realize now why people with money always look so good. It's this kind of treatment that keeps them on point," I admitted, letting go of his broad shoulders so I could look into his face. I wasn't into fronting. Duke knew I was a struggling bartender and I wasn't trying to front like I was anything other.

"It doesn't stop there, baby. We are on our way to the next phase of the plan I have for you," he said.

Damn! There was more! I thought to myself. This man had already spent some serious cake on me. What else did he have in store? We got back in the car and pulled out of the spa's parking lot.

"There can't be more. You've done enough already," I said and I was serious.

"Beautiful, you need to eat, right? This place we're going to is swanky and nice. I'm a gentleman, I would never send you home hungry," Duke said laughing.

He whipped his ride down the highway and I kept looking at him out of the corner of my eyes. He was so damn fine. We pulled into a cozy little restaurant and went inside. They seemed to know him inside. Why wasn't I not surprised? The waitress had me a little vexed the way she kept saying his name with this seductive little voice. That immediately made me suspicious that maybe Duke had something going on with her in the past.

Why are you jealous? You are here with him and she is serving you, I thought to myself, putting my mind at ease.

"What's wrong? You look a little distant," Duke asked me.

"Nothing. I'm fine," I answered, trying my best to put my suspicious thoughts out of my head.

"Good, because I have one more thing planned for you before I take you home," he told me. I almost dropped my fork when he said he had yet another thing planned for me.

"You've done more than enough Duke," I said bashfully. Honestly, I didn't want him to stop. My indifference was getting the best of me. I didn't want him to think I was a sistah that wanted him to keep doing more and more for me.

"I already told you, I planned our day down to the hour," he replied. "It's all good, baby. Trust me." And I did just that. I finally put my defenses all the way down and made myself trust Mr. Duke Carrington, businessman.

After lunch, Duke drove me all the way to the mall near the Pentagon in northern Virginia. I was shocked yet again. I didn't shop at that mall. I wasn't modest. I couldn't afford to shop at that mall. The mall had high-end stores such as Burberry and Saks Fifth Avenue. Diamond and I always talked about one day being able to shop at places like Saks Fifth Avenue and Neiman Marcus on the regular. I smirked to myself thinking about my fantasy of a personal shopper showing me dresses that cost a stack and better.

"This is the last phase of my plan for us, baby," Duke informed me. "I want you to go inside and get the prettiest dress and shoes you can find. I'm taking you to dinner tomorrow and you need the best of the best for the place we're going." I was giddy. I wanted to just throw my hands around his neck and kiss him all over his face. But I remained cool and collected as we both exited the car.

Once inside the mall, I tried to stay as calm as possible but I wanted to just run around and grab shit. We went into Saks and a lady immediately approached us.

"Mr. Carrington, you're back," the old white lady said to Duke. He smiled at her.

"Yes, Caroline. This is Lynise . . . will you help her find the perfect dress and shoes," Duke said to the lady. I watched their exchange. It was crazy that Duke had a personal shopper and he was a man . . . that was usually for women.

"Ah yes, the perfect dress and shoes," Caroline repeated, laughing.

What the fuck is so funny bitch? I retorted silently in my head. I didn't know why she was laughing and I started to feel like she was mocking me in some kind of way.

"Go ahead, Beautiful, let Caroline work her magic for you," Duke said and he took a seat on a leather chair in front of the fitting rooms.

Caroline went and got about sixty dresses for me to try on. There was every named designer you could think of. I had never, ever put my ass in a *Nicole Miller, Alexander*

McQueen, Versace or *Herve Leger* dress in my life. Caroline also brought out about thirty pairs of shoes, most of them were *Christian Louboutin*, the red bottoms I had heard Oprah Winfrey talk about and saw her wear on all of her shows.

"Damn! Beautiful, you look amazing in that shit," Duke exclaimed when I finally came out in a crimson *Herve Leger* bandage dress. He made me blush. I whirled around for him in the tight fitted dress that looked like somebody had poured me into it.

"That's the one, Beautiful . . . that is definitely the one," Duke said excitedly. That was enough for me. I went back into the fitting room and took it off. I gave it to Caroline and she and Duke rang up the dress and a pair of hot red bottoms. I came to the register just in time to see that he had paid $800 for the dress and $695 for the shoes. I felt a little nervous letting a man spend that kind of paper on me. I started thinking that Duke might expect something in return. I mean we were in a recession and this man was spending that kind of money on me. I couldn't lie to myself though, I was damn sure glad Diamond had convinced me to go out with him. Even if shit didn't work out for the long haul, this one date was well worth it.

"Here you go, baby," Duke said, handing me my bags. "All yours," he smiled.

"Oh my goodness, Duke, I cannot thank you enough for such a wonderful first date," I said and gave him a hug and a kiss on his cheek. I released him just in time to see Caroline smirking. I rolled my eyes at the old white bag. I told myself that bitch was just jealous. Maybe she wanted Duke too, just like the fucking waitress did.

"So you want me to drop you back at the Marriot or to where you live," Duke said snidely as we pulled back around my neighborhood.

"Well . . . um . . . you can take me home. The reason I—" I started to explain, but Duke cut me off.

"Baby, it's all good. I was real happy when you didn't give me your address right away. That told me you were smarter than most of these chicks out here," Duke interjected. I felt a sense of relief that he understood. Then I told him my address.

Duke pulled up in front of my apartment complex and I prepared to leave the car. He leaned over and kissed me softly on my cheek. I almost fucking melted inside.

"I will see you tomorrow night when you put that dress on," he said in a low whisper. I wanted to tongue him down so badly. I swallowed the lump in my throat.

"Yes, I will see you tomorrow. Thank you again for a more than wonderful day," I said softly. Then I kissed him back, also on the cheek.

I exited the car and flew up the stairs to my apartment. I rushed inside and called out for Diamond. "Diamond! Dee, you here?" I hollered. I raced into her bedroom but it was empty. Then I looked at the cable box, it was nine o'clock. Diamond was probably at the club already, I reasoned. Then it dawned on me that I hadn't called Neeko to let him know I was going to be late for fucking work.

"Shit!" I cursed myself and went to pick up my cell phone. I dialed Diamond's cell first. I wanted her to tell me if Neeko had asked for me or find out what kind of mood he was in. Diamond's phone went straight to voicemail. "She must be on the damn phone with that bastard Brian," I mumbled.

I clicked off and went to dial Diamond's number again. I flopped down on our raggedy couch and started to press send on my phone. Suddenly, I looked over at the Saks bag and said fuck it. I didn't bother to call Diamond again. I figured I would just see her when she got home. I was no longer worried about Neeko's ass. "I will just show up tomorrow if I feel like it. Neeko don't be paying a bitch anyway and those fucking tips suck nowadays," I told myself.

I picked up my Saks bag and put on my new shoes and strutted around my apartment feeling like a star.

"I might just be quitting that fucking job soon anyway, when I become Mrs. Duke Carrington," I said out loud, *smiling from ear to ear.*

CHAPTER 4
SHE'S COMING HOME WITH ME

I had fallen asleep waiting up for Diamond.

When I got up the next day, she was knocked out sleeping and I figured she had a hard night at the club, so I chose not to wake her. As bad as I wanted to shake her ass and show her the dress and the shoes, I didn't bother. I had some running around to do since I knew Duke was taking me out that night. This time, I wanted to accent the dress with the perfect hairdo, so I called up my girls at the Beauty R Us Hair and Nail Salon and told my hairdresser I was coming. I knew it was going to be an all day affair because the hair salon was more like a social gathering.

I took a shower and threw on a Juicy sweat suit. I checked in on Diamond and she was still out like a light. I scribbled a note down telling her to call me on my cell when she got up and then I grabbed my purse and headed out.

When I got to the salon, I noticed a missed call from Duke. I smiled wide. It was so good that he had been the first to call after our date and not me. Duke was showing so much damn husband potential I couldn't take it.

I immediately called him back while I sat in the car waiting for my hairdresser to summon me inside.

"Hey, Beautiful," he answered. I couldn't help but smile. He told me to be ready by seven-thirty, which gave me plenty of time to get my hair done, shower and get dressed. I told him I would be ready when he got there.

When I got home from the hair salon, Diamond had already gotten up and left the house. "Damn! Why she ain't call me back? I know she had to see all the missed calls from me," I grumbled to myself. I started getting my shit ready to get dressed. Then I thought about how the hell I was going to do my make-up without Diamond. Shaking my head, I picked up the phone and tried her one last time. Her phone went straight to voicemail once again. "Diamond, it's me. Call my cell as soon as you get this message," I said with attitude.

I got dressed for my date with Duke and I was starting to get real worried about Diamond. Even after my message she still had not called me back. I had called her at least ten times. Sometimes it rang but most times it went straight to voicemail. I kept looking at my watch hoping she would come home before I had to leave. I lied to myself and said primarily because she had skills in the make-up department, but I was worried about her as well.

I pranced around the apartment for a while in my new dress and shoes and I had to admit that I looked damned good. Finally, it was time for Duke to pick me up. I was forced to put on my own make-up and Diamond never came home to tell me how I looked. "Oh well, Diamond, I tried to wait for your ass. I'm gonna curse you out when I see you," I said out loud as if Diamond was there. Really, I was trying to appease myself. I was pissed with her. I knew for sure her neglect had something to do with Brian. He was probably out of the hospital and taking up all of her time. At least that's what I told myself.

When Duke pulled up to my complex, I was peeking out of my window. I looked at my watch and decided I would make him wait for a good five or ten minutes before I came outside. It was a little payback for him making me wait the day before. Besides, I wanted to make a grand appearance, so me waiting outside was not an option.

I let my grace period pass and then I headed outside. When I emerged in the parking lot, Duke rolled his window down and whistled, which caused me to smile.

"Mmm, mmm, mmm, Beautiful, you look delicious in that dress," Duke called out to me as I made my way to the car. He had gotten out and opened my door.

"Thank you, Mr. Carrington," I commented, as I slid into my seat. Duke kept giving me compliments as he drove to the restaurant. I think he must've made me blush fifty times.

We pulled up to the Melting Pot, one of the most expensive restaurants in Virginia Beach. Once again, Duke was about to do it big. He drove his Porsche 911 up to the valet stand and stopped. This time I waited in my seat until he opened the door for me. He helped me out and held my hand while he gave his keys to the valet guy. Duke didn't let my hand go the entire time it took us to walk into the Melting Pot and get our table. Once at the table, he pulled out my chair and pushed it up to the table once I sat down.

We began our nice, quiet and romantic dinner with a toast to us. The expensive champagne caused a tingling in my throat and eased my mind. I must've had five glasses of champagne before we completed dinner. I was tipsy as hell by the time the valet brought the car around. I was holding onto Duke's muscular arm for dear life.

"You ok?" he asked me.

"I'm fine," I lied. I really didn't drink like that so the champagne had snuck up on me. Once the car came, we drove and I didn't even ask Duke where we were going. I just rested my head back on the headrest and went along with whatever else he had planned.

I had my eyes closed when we finally stopped moving. "Beautiful, we're here," Duke said, touching the side of my face gently. I popped my eyes open, embarrassed that I had drifted off. I looked out the window and noticed a huge house in front of me. I looked over at Duke with a confused look on my face. He started chuckling.

"This is my house," he said.

I relaxed a bit. I was still kind of out of it, but my buzz was wearing off a little bit. I followed Duke into his grand home. The shit was off the chain. I estimated in my head that the house had to be at least 3,000 square feet. We started walking through it and I noticed immediately all of the expensive furniture, artwork and home décor. Once we were in his living room, I looked out the huge glass bay window and noticed the beach. Duke had one of the coveted nicest properties in Virginia Beach. "This is nice," I said, staring out the window.

"This is only one of my homes," Duke volunteered. "I don't stay here most of the time. I have a few places here and there."

He sat down on an all-white leather couch and put his feet up on a glass coffee table. "Come over here and sit with me," Duke instructed, patting a spot on the couch next to him. I turned around from the window and smiled at him.

"Gladly," I said seductively. I eased onto the couch next to Duke and he wrapped his strong arm around my shoulder and pulled me as close to him as I could go. I rested my head on his shoulder and sighed.

"Did you have a good time tonight?" he asked me.

I lifted my head a little, so I could look at him. "No," I said and paused. He crinkled his face. "I had a wonderful, magnificent, awesome time," I said, then I let a big smile spread across my face. Duke's face eased into a smile.

"Whew, you had me scared there for a minute," he said jokingly, acting like he was wiping sweat off his forehead. We sat there for a few minutes like that. Then Duke excused himself and left the room for a minute. He came back with just his wife beater holding a chilled bottle of champagne and two flutes. I couldn't stop staring at his ripped abs and beautiful chest through his undershirt. He knew his ass was fine too.

Duke placed the flutes down and poured us each a glass of champagne. I started to tell him no, but I didn't want to rock the boat. We were having such a great time together. I picked up my flute and he did the same. We each took a sip and Duke busted out laughing at my reaction to the bubbly. "This expensive shit takes some getting used to," he smirked.

After two glasses of the strong bubbly, I was feeling my head sway once again. Duke moved real close to me and took the flute out of my hand. My heart was beating uncontrollably as I felt his body heat next to me. He put the flute on the coffee table and turned back to me. I didn't know what to do. Duke reached out and grabbed my face in his hands and brought it close to his. Instinctively, I closed my eyes. Duke placed his sweet tasting lips on top of mine and we began kissing savagely. He tasted so good. I could feel myself growing hot and my pussy getting wet. Duke moved in closer and I could feel his dick hard against my pelvis. We continued kissing. Then Duke put his hand on my breast through my dress and squeezed slightly. I let out a short gasp. My mind started to clear. I started getting nervous. Somewhere in my mind I was back in high school attempting to have sex for the first time. Duke's hands were starting to travel to different places on my body and that made me uneasy, but brought me back to the here and now. My buzz was fading rapidly. When Duke started unzipping my dress, I pushed him off me.

He stopped abruptly.

I sat up and wiped my lips. Then I stood up and pulled my dress back down over my hips as it had ridden all the way up during our hot patting session.

"What's wrong, Beautiful?" Duke asked, sounding kind of out of breath. I knew he was horny and ready to fuck. "Nothing. It's just early for—" I started.

"Baby, whether you give it to me the first time or the tenth time, I am a gentleman," Duke said, interrupting me in mid-sentence in his attempt to convince me it would be all right.

"Well, I'm not one of those easy chicks. I'd rather wait," I told him. I was still standing up.

He reached out and pulled me back down to him. It was as if he wasn't trying to take no for an answer. Duke roughly put his mouth on top of mine again and forced his tongue into my mouth. This time it didn't taste as good as the first time. I felt as if he was trying to choke me. I started squirming and then I forcefully pushed him. I couldn't move his muscular body, but he eventually got the picture and stopped holding me down. I stood up again. Between the effects of the champagne and my heavy breathing from trying to get Duke off me, I felt a little dizzy. I staggered away from him.

"Beautiful, I'm sorry. I'm just feeling you so much," he explained. I softened when he said that.

"I just don't want to do it right now, Duke. Please understand," I said. I wanted him to respect me. He could say whatever he wanted to say, if I had let him fuck me so soon he wouldn't want to make me his wifey. I was trying to be somebody's wife, not go through another quick, *slam-bam-thank you ma'am* relationship.

Duke was quiet. He looked like he was disappointed. I wanted to rush over to him and beg him to understand but I stood my ground instead. I was almost sure he probably had women all over Virginia, but I wanted to win him over. I wanted to be with him for the long haul if it was meant to be. If I had given in to him that early, I knew that would be the kiss of death for my chances at being his number one.

"Duke, are you ok?" I asked as I picked up my purse.

"I'm good. I will take you home as soon as my head clears a little bit," he said flatly. I could tell he was really disappointed by the situation.

"It's all good. I can take a cab home. I have to go anyway. Diamond doesn't have her keys and I need to let her in the house," I lied. I needed to get the heck out of there as fast as possible before I gave in to him. I wanted him but I had to stand pat. To give in would be the end of my dream.

Surprisingly, Duke didn't argue with me. Instead, he was good enough to call me a cab. He tried to give me money for the cab, but since I was the one who insisted on taking a cab, I refused his money. He grabbed my purse and pushed the money inside. I was glad. Truth be told, from where Duke lived to where I lived was going to be expensive and I had only brought forty dollars with me.

When the cab arrived, I told Duke good night. He didn't try to kiss me or anything. I hung my head and walked to the cab.

I looked back at Duke when the cab pulled out of his driveway. He was still watching me, which told me although he was disappointed that I didn't give it up, he was probably impressed with the fact that he would have to work hard to get me.

I wanted to be a lady of class for him.

CHAPTER 5
SOME PEOPLE HATE

I dialed Diamond's phone as soon as I got in the cab. Diamond finally answered her damn phone. "What's up? Where the hell you been at?" I yelled into the receiver, causing the cab driver to look at me funny. I frowned at his ass and continued with my conversation. Diamond gave me some lame ass excuse about she was at the club, then she went here and there. The bottom line after all the bullshit was that she was caught up with Brian because he had gotten out of the hospital.

"Well, I forgive you this time. But don't do that shit again! You had me fucking worried like hell," I chastised. Diamond promised not to disappear like that. Then she asked me for all of the details about me and Duke.

"Diamond, you don't understand how much I am feeling this nigga," I told her. I could tell by the screeching in the phone that Diamond was excited for me. She made me smile.

45 | CHEAPER *to* KEEP HER

I told her all about the spa, lunch, shopping, the dress and all of it. She told me she had seen the Saks bags. Then I told her about what had just happened with Duke. "Girl, I feel so guilty not giving him some after all the shit he did for me these last two days," I said sadly.

"Don't you feel guilty girl. He can wait and the longer you make him wait, the more respect he gon' have for that ass," Diamond told me sternly.

"You think so?" I questioned, sounding unsure. I was usually the one giving her advice and now I was so sprung over Duke the tables had turned.

"Yes! Nini, listen to ya girl. If I were you, I would make him wait two more fucking dates. If a nigga really wants you, he will wait," Diamond told me. I was listening to her and I loved her for making me feel better. But after seeing Duke sit back on his couch with a hard dick and an attitude, I didn't know how much longer I could make him wait for the pussy before he would just move on to the next one. Duke was powerful and had money, which meant he could have any bitch anywhere.

Diamond and I spoke for almost my entire ride home. She promised me she would be in the house when I got there and we would continue our conversation.

I paid the cab driver and climbed the stairs to my apartment. As soon as I got near the door, I heard a loud commotion coming from inside. I couldn't get my key out fast enough. That's when I heard Diamond screaming. With my hands shaking, I finally got the key in the door and pushed the door open. I heard another loud scream coming from Diamond's bedroom and then a bunch of thumping and banging.

"What the fuck!" I gasped. I kicked off my pumps and ran to Diamond's door. It was locked. "Diamond! Diamond, open the door!" I screamed banging on the door. She screamed again, this time I heard her pleading for Brian to stop.

"This muthafucka!" I screamed, banging my body up against the door. That shit didn't budge. I started kicking the door frantically and screaming. Finally, the door banged open. I saw Brian choking Diamond and then he slapped her across her face.

"Bitch, you stole my fucking drugs!" he barked and hit her again.

I raced into the room and jumped right on Brian's back. "Get off her you fucking bitch ass nigga!" I screamed at the top of my lungs.

Brian let go of Diamond and tried to get me off his back. Diamond was on the floor gasping for air. "Get the fuck off me, you ugly bitch!" Brian said to me, as he spun around trying to get me off of him. I dug my nails into his neck and slid off him. I then punched and kicked him. He tried to grab my wrists but I was too fast for his ass. He swung on me but miss. My dress was all the way up over my hips but I didn't even care. I was gonna fuck Brian up for putting his hands on my best friend. I was finally sick of his shit.

"You no good piece of shit," I charged at him again. This time Diamond jumped in the way. She was crying hysterically.

"Lynise! Stop! Don't hit him no more!" Diamond cried out. That shit stopped me dead in my tracks. I looked at Diamond like she was fucking smoking crack.

"Oh, you protecting this bitch ass nigga after he was in here trying to kill you?" I hollered at her, my chest rising and falling rapidly.

"It's my fault Lynise. Just stay out of it," Diamond said firmly. Her words were like a slap in my face. I couldn't understand what this bitch could possibly see in this nigga, especially now that he was beating her ass.

"You are a stupid ass if you stay with his bitch nigga and let him beat on you Diamond!" I tried screaming wisdom in her dense mind. "You're right, it ain't none of my fucking business, just don't call me when this no good ass bum tries to kill your ass again!"

"Just get out! Everybody ain't like the rich nigga you fucking with! You better not forget where you came from!" Diamond screamed back in response.

I couldn't believe her words. She sounded like a jealous enemy instead of my best friend. I was shut down. I pulled my dress down and backed out of her room. "Let that nigga kill you then," I said out of anger. I knew I didn't mean it, but I was fucking seething mad.

Diamond slammed the door in my face and left me standing outside of her room. I was devastated by her treatment. From then on, I started living for Lynise. I took on a *fuck it* attitude. Diamond would just have to make her own way. She was right . . . there weren't many men out there like Duke and I was going to make sure I kept him.

Chapter 6
Streets Are Talking

I had a lot of shit on my mind the next day after the dust up with Diamond and Brian.

To top it off, I had not heard from Duke. He hadn't answered my calls all day. I was starting to feel like I had messed up a good thing just because I didn't give him some ass. I decided to call Neeko and beg him to let me come to the *Magic City* to work. I hadn't shown up in the two days that I went out with Duke. Yeah, I had to admit that I got a bit carried away thinking he was going to take care of me and I didn't need to work. In any case, Neeko was glad to let me come in to work because he said mad customers had been complaining about weak drinks while I wasn't there. I was glad to hear that my boss appreciated the way I worked.

I was so excited that I left the house without knocking on Diamond's door to ask her if she wanted to ride with me. Now that Brian was around she was probably going to be missing work anyway. When I got to the club, shit looked slow. It was late and there was only about half of the regular customers there. I slid behind the bar and prepared myself to work. When I got settled in I looked out into the crowd and noticed J-Rock, a dude I had grown up with and kicked it with off and on for years. He was bopping over to the bar. I smiled and he smiled back.

"What's up shawty?" J-Rock said with his southern drawl.

"Ain't shit but this work," I replied.

"I hear you, I hear you," he said.

"What can I get you tonight?" I asked. Shit, I needed to mix something and get some tips in my jar.

"Lemme just get a shot of that Henn dog. You know my usual, why you playing?"

"You're right, I forgot for a minute," I chuckled. I got him his Hennessey and he took it back in a flash.

"Lemme get another one shawty. A nigga gotta get his mind right up in this camp tonight," he told me. I did as he asked. Another little swig of Hennessey was in front of J-Rock with the quickness.

He ordered two more drinks and we talked. It was kind of slow at the bar so I could give him my attention. J-Rock started telling me all his business once he had a few drinks. All his baby mama drama and about how niggas in the streets were snitching on each other. I just listened. He was my entertainment and he was keeping my mind off my double drama—Duke and Diamond. I didn't mind J-Rock's stories at all. He was definitely a welcomed relief.

J-Rock's and my conversation was interrupted when a tall, dark skinned dude walked into the *Magic City*. I had never seen the man before and he was ugly as hell. The guy started waving to get J-Rock's attention. "Um . . . that dude is calling you," I told J-Rock who had his back turned to the club's door.

J-Rock turned around slowly and it seemed like he immediately recognized the guy. "Lynise, it was sweet talking to you ma. I gotta go holla at this cat," J-Rock told me as he placed two twenty dollar bills on the bar.

I smiled at him. "Go handle yours boo," I said, picking up the tip with the quickness.

J-Rock walked over to the guy, gave him a pound and they headed straight for the men's bathroom. That was kind of strange to me, but I put the thought out of my mind and focused back in on trying to make more drinks and in turn make more tips. Normally, my attention would be elsewhere but the night was slow and my attention span was keen to my surroundings.

Not even five minutes after J-Rock and the hideous stranger disappeared into the bathroom I heard a loud crashing sound coming from the front door. "What the hell?" I huffed and before I could even react I heard what no club owner wants to hear, "Police! Everybody on the ground now! Police! Get the fuck down!"

I put my hands up in the air in response to the cops' loud demands. It was the Virginia state police narcotics squad. They had their guns drawn and were grabbing people throwing them to the floor. I moved slowly from behind the bar with my hands in the air so they would know I didn't have a weapon of any kind.

"Everybody in the middle of the floor on your stomachs now!" one of the narcotics cops yelled.

I could hear Neeko yelling, "What the fuck is going on? Why the fuck ya'll up in my place? We ain't done shit!" The cops threw his ass down on the floor too. Neeko, all the strippers, whether they were naked or had on clothes, all of the customers and me were lying on the floor. I saw four of the cops going towards the men's bathroom and I immediately thought about J-Rock. He was so cool I wished I could have warned him. But I couldn't and it was too late.

They busted down the bathroom door. "The drugs are right in here!" one of the cops yelled with his nine millimeter in hand.

"I'll be damned," I mumbled. J-Rock was fucking selling drugs to that ugly dude who was probably an undercover narc and the reason for the raid. Neeko was pissed, I could tell. It took a while but they eventually hauled J-Rock out of the restroom in handcuffs. He held his head down in shame. Then some of the narcotics cops came over to where we were all laying and they grabbed up a dude from the floor.

"Where's the fucking gun?" one of the cops yelled at the dude. The dude just lifted his shirt and right there in his waistband was a pistol. He was arrested too. They got Neeko up off the floor and led him into the back to his office. I guess they wanted to question him about the goings on in his club. I was sick of being down on that fucking dirty floor at gunpoint but finally the cops that had been talking to Neeko came back out.

"Everybody needs to stay down on the floor until we are all out the door," one of the cops yelled to us. People started sucking their teeth and groaning, but everybody listened. Nobody was trying to get shot. The cops started to file out. They were walking backwards towards the doors with their guns still out. There was no way they were going to take their eyes off any of us. When the last narco was out the door, we all started to get up off the floor. I brushed off my clothes and listened to all the customers and working girls start speculating about who was the snitch that had caused the raid. I heard one of the customers say, "it must've been that nigga that went in the bathroom with J-Rock."

Another man agreed saying that nobody had ever seen him in the club before. Some of the club's regulars started complaining to Neeko and telling him that he needed to be more selective about who he let up in the club.

All the fucking chaos and now the talking, plus Duke not calling and Diamond being mad at me had me stressed the fuck out. I walked my ass back to the bar shaking my head. With my hands still shaking, I picked up a shot glass and a bottle of premium Patron. I poured myself a shot, picked up a slice of lemon and took that fucking shot to the head. I hurried up and sucked on the lemon to counteract the strong tequila. It burned going down, but I needed it right now. Neeko was trying to get people to stay in the club and spend money but muthfuckas was trying to get far the hell away from the *Magic City* right now. I couldn't blame them.

Pretty soon the club was almost completely empty. Even the strippers started taking the rest of the night off. The DJ started packing up his shit too. In the time the police had shut the club down, mad people had gotten turned away, which meant I wasn't going to make any money anyway.

I looked around and decided I was going to head out with everybody else. Shit, wasn't any use in wasting my damn time there. Another night of bullshit at the *Magic City*. Once again some shit had jumped off and I didn't make much money in tips. I was pissed the fuck off. Coming to the club night in and night out was getting less and less worth it. I was tired of the bullshit—at the club, with Diamond and with my fucking life.

"I ain't gon' be able to take much more of this shit around here at this club. I don't know if they ever gon' see my ass again," I said out loud as I snatched my purse and stomped towards the door.

Chapter 7
Ain't No Ngga Like the One I Got

After all the drama in the club I just wanted to get as far away as possible.

When I got outside and headed to my car I heard a horn tooting behind me. At first I ignored it but then I heard gravel crunching as the car pulled up aside me. "Hey, Beautiful, why you leaving work so early?" a familiar voice called out.

It was Duke! My heart immediately started pumping fast. I was kind of shocked to see him there since I thought he had written me off. I quickly put that shock aside and showed Duke that I was more than happy to see him.

"There was major drama up in there tonight. I just can't do it no more. I don't know what I'm gonna do about a job, but I can't take the bullshit that be going on up in there," I said sadly.

"Come with me and let me take your mind off this shit here," Duke suggested.

"How? What? But I have my car here," I stammered. I was caught off guard by his offer to take me away from the club.

"Beautiful, in a few you ain't gon' need that hoopty," he replied. "You damn sure ain't gonna need no fucking bartending job. Especially if you keep looking as good as you do. Now get ya ass in here and ride," Duke said laughing afterwards.

I busted out laughing and blushed at the same time. Duke was so charming. I gladly slid my ass in his car and when I was all the way in the seat I exhaled.

"So tell me all about what happened up in there tonight," Duke said as he peeled out of the Magic City's parking lot. I started telling Duke about the raid and everything that happened. I even had enough time to get into what had happened between me and Diamond. He told me that good friendships were hard to find and that I shouldn't let a man come between me and my best friend. He was right about that. I promised to call her and make up with her as soon as I had a free minute.

I was so into the conversation with Duke that I wasn't watching where we were driving to. I was so happy he had surprisingly pick me up. I started thinking this man really must like me a lot. I got kind of angry when I started thinking about Diamond telling me to make him wait longer. I now realized from her statement during our argument that she was just jealous that Duke, a man of substance, wanted me and not her. I had made it up in my mind that the next time he went for the ass, I would give it to him. *Fuck what Diamond was talking about!* I screamed inside my head.

My jaw almost dropped when Duke pulled up to the exclusive Cosmopolitan building in the heart of Virginia Beach. "What's here?" I asked, looking up at the building.

Duke smiled. "I live here too. I told you I have a few places to live here and there," Duke said, pulling his car into his reserved spot. He got out and I waited. Sure enough, he opened my door and helped me out of his car. We went into the beautiful condominium building. It was such a nice, clean, upscale building. Not like my ghetto-ass apartment complex. When we got on the elevator, Duke pressed five and then turned his attention to me.

"C'mere, Beautiful. I missed not speaking to you for all that time. We can't be doing shit like that again . . . I don't want you to stay away from me ever," he said sexily.

He placed his hand under my chin and pushed it upwards towards his face. I lifted my face to his in response. He looked into my eyes and I closed them. Duke then bent down and placed his lips on top of mine. I opened my mouth slightly, accepting his tongue. It tasted so sweet like cinnamon Altoids. We moved our tongues in and out of each other's mouths rapidly. Our breathing became labored and I could tell we were both growing hot in our pants. We kissed passionately until the elevator door dinged and opened on Duke's floor. He pulled away from me and urged me out of the door.

"Damn girl, you make a nigga wanna get married. Your ass is fine as hell and you can kiss," Duke said almost breathlessly. His sweet words sent a funny feeling down my spine. I had never had a man even mention marriage and my name in the same sentence. Niggas in the 'hood that I was used to messing with weren't trying to hear shit about marriage. Duke just didn't know how much I was feeling him too.

He led me down the end of the hallway to his condo. Prior to putting the key in the door he pushed me up against it and started kissing me again. I was loving every minute of it. I wrapped my arms around his neck and caressed the back of his head while I feverishly returned his kiss. His skin was smooth and buttery. He smelled good and his body was strong, like a real man should be.

He rubbed his hands over my chest and when he felt my nipples were rock hard he squeezed them slightly. That shit made me gasp. Now I could tell my pussy was soaking wet. Everything about Duke was intoxicating. I couldn't think straight. "Let's go inside," I said, moving away from his kiss.

Duke smiled at me seductively. "A'ight, baby, but I don't know what a nigga will do to you once we get inside. You got me on swell," he said. Then he put the key in the door and we stumbled inside. He stopped for a minute and punched some numbers into a keypad. I guess it was the alarm. Duke didn't waste any time turning his attention back to me. He held my hand and led me to the same type of expensive leather sectional that he had in his other house. I was yet impressed me with yet another of his homes.

The condo was decorated in an art deco style with all the furniture having that ultra modern look. However, one thing struck me as strange. Looking around the condo, I didn't notice any photographs or signs that the house was his. Even stranger, I noticed the same thing at his other house. Just expensive artwork on the walls and every type of high priced electronics you could imagine. I started wondering why none of Duke's homes were personalized with little signs of him. No shoes lying around, no pictures, nothing that said he lived at either location. I looked at his fine ass and quickly put my paranoid thoughts out of my mind. I wasn't trying to drive myself crazy thinking negative thoughts about Duke. I decided to go with the flow when it came to him.

"Wait right here. I'm gonna get us something to drink to cool us down," Duke said jokingly. His ass knew he was the one who really needed cooling down. I could still see his rock hard dick through his pants when he stood up. I just nodded. I don't know who had told him I wanted to be cooled down. I wanted to tell him fuck the drink, come back and get this, but I played it cool.

When Duke disappeared to get the drinks I looked down at the magazines on the coffee table and flipped through a few of them. I quickly scanned GQ and Essence before I noticed copies of Woman's Health and Vogue magazines. My face crinkled at that the sight of the women magazines. *Why would a single man have copies of girly magazines?* Girly magazines that weren't porn. Duke surely didn't look like the type to read that kind of material. I heard Duke's footsteps so I hurriedly put the women's magazines back under the pile. That shit was bothering me, but I wouldn't have dared questioned him. I was nowhere near that status with him yet, but I surely did make a mental note to myself.

"Here you go, Beautiful," Duke said, handing me a beautiful crystal glass with a pink drink in it.

Being the drink connoisseur that I am, I sniffed the drink and said, "This is Nuvo, huh?"

Duke laughed at me. "Damn you're good," he said.

"I love Nuvo. Thank you," I replied, lifting the glass to my lips and taking a sip. Duke slid down on the couch next to me. He took a swig of his drink as well. "You have really beautiful homes, Duke," I complimented.

"I try. I'm really into real estate. I came up in the 'hood in Virginia Beach, barely having a place to live, knocking from pillar to post so I wanted to buy as much good property as possible, feel me?" Duke explained.

It was the first time he ever revealed anything about himself to me. "Yeah, I can relate. I didn't have an easy childhood myself," I reported.

I had to take another sip of my drink just thinking about some of the shit I had endured as a child. My mother was a mean bitch and she never gave me shit. When I turned fifteen she told me I had to go because she had a new man and she thought he would be more attracted to me than to her. I had been on my own since then, knocking from place to place.

"Hey, the past is the past. To new beginnings," Duke said, lifting his glass and tapping against mine in a toast. He got me to stop thinking about my bitch of a mother.

"Yup, to brand new beginnings," I whispered seductively.

I think that was enough for Duke. He downed his drink and so did I. Then we turned our attention to each other. Duke came close to me and placed his hand behind my head. I closed my eyes as he ran his fingers through my naturally long hair. No weaves or wigs for me. I think that was something he liked the most about me. He had told me on our first date that he always preferred natural women.

"You are so fine," he said as he drew his hand from my hair. I opened my mouth to reply but Duke quickly stuck his tongue inside of it. We kissed like two animals in heat again. He finally moved his lips off of mine and began licking down my neck. Oh God! I couldn't take that shit. My neck was one of my weak spots. I started squirming as the hot feeling in my loins caused me to wanna just grind my hips.

Duke pressed against me and I could feel his rock hard dick against my pelvis. I began grinding my hips upward towards his dick trying to press my clit on his rock hard shit. I wanted him to know that I wanted to feel him inside of me real bad. Duke lifted my shirt and with one touch he had the front clasp on my bra loosened. He had skills. My size C cup breasts jumped loose and Duke put his mouth on my nipples. "Ohhh," I sang out. The heat from his mouth was sending me over the top. He sucked on my nipples so hard he caused me to grind harder and faster. It felt so good I had to move my head side-to-side. Each time I moved, Duke sucked harder and harder. I couldn't control myself.

"I want you!" I screamed out.

My pussy was soaking wet. I could feel the moisture in my panties. Duke stood up abruptly and hovered over me. I looked up at him with innocent eyes. He quickly unbuttoned my jeans and pulled them down over my hips and all the way off. The cool air on my clit made me feel hot as hell. I spread my legs open so Duke could get a good look at my creamy pussy. Any inhibitions I had previously had about sleeping with him early were gone.

"Damn, that is a pretty pussy! Mmmm, mmm," Duke complimented. I reached down and put my index finger in my pussy. I fingered my pussy, sliding my finger in and out, enticing Duke.

"Shit!" he moaned, grabbing his dick through his pants. Then he did some shit that surprised me. He dropped to his knees in front of me and put his face between my legs.

"Ahhh," I screamed out. Duke started darting his tongue into my hole real fast, in and out. "Oh God! Oh God! Oh God!" I hollered. My moans just drove him crazier. Duke made loud slurping noises while he ate the shit out of my pussy. I was pumping my ass, shoving that pussy at his tongue.

"C'mon . . . give it to me," I told him. Duke got up and slid out of his jeans. His legs were so toned and his dick hung almost to his knees. I licked my lips but before I could go down on him, Duke hoisted me up and held me against him. I put my legs up around his waist and straddled him. I held onto his neck so I wouldn't fall while he guided his dick into my pussy.

"Owww!" I screamed when he put his thick, solid dick into me. Duke flopped back on the couch and now I was riding him. I bounced up and down on that dick so hard and fast he was breathing like he had just run laps. "Oh, fuck me! Fuck me good," I talked much shit while I rode that dick.

"Oh shit, girl, your pussy is out of this fucking world," Duke growled. Just when I thought he was going to cum, I jumped up off his dick. "Wait...where you goin'?" he said, looking as if he was about to beg me to get back on it.

I laughed.

Then I turned around and got back on his dick backwards so he could see my whole ass, *the reverse cowgirl*. No man worth his salt could turn this shit down. Seeing a woman in this position made men's dicks harder and added to the throbbing sensation. I knew this shit even before I started working at the Magic City. But I could see the men's mouths salivating when the dancers turned their asses around, giving the patrons quite a fucking show.

I bent over at the waist and pumped up and down on his dick again. "Awww fuck!" he moaned. Duke slapped my ass cheeks as I fucked the shit out of him. I planted my feet for leverage and then I used both of my hands and spread my ass cheeks apart so he could see his dick go in and out of my pussy. "I see it! Fuck me! I see it!" Duke called out. This was what us women live for—to drive a muthafucka crazy tapping that ass. The ultimate in pussy whipping.

I started to feel myself about to cum because the shaft of his dick was pressing on my g-spot. "I'm coming!" I called out and then I sat up, closed my legs together and squeezed his dick with my pussy.

"Agggghhhh!" Duke bucked and screamed. He was coming as well. I jumped up quickly but I think some of his cum had got inside of me. I turned around and he started jerking the rest of his cum onto my tits. That turned Duke on even more. "Goddamn girl, that was some bomb ass pussy," Duke gasped. He started rubbing his dick and I watched it start to grow hard again.

"C'mere . . . we ain't finished yet," he said. Pulling me back down onto him, Duke and I went for rounds two, three and even, four. We finally ended up in his king sized bed where I collapsed from exhaustion. He kept telling me repeatedly how good my pussy was. I even remember him saying I was the best he ever had.

The next morning when I got up Duke had already gotten out of the bed. I lifted my head to see if he was in the room and that is when I heard him out in the living room talking. He was calm at first, then I heard his voice rise, then he got calm again. I couldn't make out what he was saying and I damn sure didn't want to eavesdrop, so I laid back down.

I looked around the huge bedroom with all the pretty accessories and wished I never had to leave here and go home to my cramped little apartment. I exhaled deeply and said a silent prayer that it wouldn't be much longer before Duke and I got exclusive and serious. Before we fucked I didn't want to press the issue and ask him if he had a girl or women that he fucked . . . I was sure he did. But now that I had taken that step with him my mind was racing with ways to approach the topic with him. I mean, what would I say, "Tell me who you fucking?"

Finally, it sounded like Duke had gotten off the phone. I quickly turned on my side and pretended to still be asleep. He walked into the room and climbed on the bed. He leaned over me, pulled my hair behind my ear and began kissing my neck. I knew what that meant. "Mmm," I moaned, pretending I was just waking up from his touch.

He gently pulled me by the shoulder until I was on my back. I arched my back sexily and stretched. I opened my eyes and smiled at him. "Good morning," I mumbled, still acting like he'd awaken me from a deep sleep. Duke didn't say anything. His face was like stone. But he wedged his way between my legs and drove his dick right into me. "Ahh!" I sighed.

He started fucking me hard and fast like he wanted to punish me and my pussy first thing in the morning. I grabbed at his muscular back and dug my nails deep into it. That caused him to punish my pussy even more. He fucked me harder and harder. I thought he would send me through the bed.

"Oh yeah . . . I like it rough! Fuck me! Fuck it! Fuck that pussy!" I started talking shit. I knew that would turn him on. Sure enough, Duke pulled out of me and jerked his dick in my direction. Cum shot everywhere. I think some even got in my hair. "Yeah, daddy," I said, sounding like a porn star. Duke fell down next to me on the bed. I turned towards him and started stroking his head and rubbing his back. There was no place I wanted to be, then right there.

"Beautiful, I think you should stay here . . . you know, move the fuck up out of that 'hood rat shit hole and just stay here," Duke said nonchalantly. I was speechless at what I heard. I was overwhelmed with joy but yet still speechless. "You hear me? I know it's early, but I think I want you around all the time. Fuck that job, fuck that apartment . . . I want you to be at my disposal."

I heard the seriousness in his voice. I wanted to think about my answer but it seemed as if my impulses reacted before I could really think things through. "Hell yeah! Yes, daddy! I will stay here. I will quit and I will be yours whenever and wherever you want me to be," I said, climbing on top of him to fuck him again. He stopped me before I could get on his dick.

"I'm sorry but I gotta go," he said. He pushed me off him and got out of the bed. I sat Indian style on the bed with a long face. Duke turned on the shower in the bathroom as I sat there. Before he got in the shower, he walked over to his dresser and picked up a set of keys. He tossed them on the bed.

"Those are yours for your new home," he said. The keys landed right next to my legs. I looked down at them and then back at him. I really felt like crying tears of joy. "The alarm code is on the fridge. Learn it because if you forget they will come storming over here."

"Ok," I replied.

"I got a meeting to go to so I will be gone for a while," Duke explained. "I can't get calls where I'm going, so just wait to hear from me. There's cash up there on the dresser. Go shopping, get whatever you want. Just make sure you answer when I call." With that he walked into the bathroom and slammed the door.

I flopped back on the bed and kicked my legs. "Yes! Yes! Yes!" I excitedly whispered to myself. I started singing, *Ain't no nigga like the one I got!*

I was going to be with Duke Carrington forever . . . or so I thought.

CHAPTER 8
LET ME UPGRADE YOU

I played it very cool until Duke left the condo for a meeting.

He had kissed me deep and passionately and told me he would be returning for more. He left me with a wad of cash and keys to the hot ass condo. He had me. Hook, line and fucking sinker. I would've married him that day if he had asked me to.

When I finally heard the door slam behind him I jumped up off the bed and picked up my cell phone. Mad or not, there was no other person I would call besides my BFF, my best friend forever, Diamond.

She answered on the first ring. "Hello, I'm sorry," I blurted out. Funny and ironically, Diamond said the same exact thing at the same exact time. She started explaining to me that she was just uptight over the fight with Brian and that she would never pick Brian over me. Needless to say she and I made up on the phone. That's how good of friends we were. We always made up fast whenever we had a falling out over bullshit.

"Ok, enough of the sappy, sorry bullshit. Girl! Guess where I'm at!" I screeched excitedly into the phone. Diamond told me she was listening. "Diamond! I am in a fucking beautiful fifth floor condo in the Cosmo building!" I reported in a high-pitched voice. Diamond was screaming on the other end.

"Wait . . . wait . . . girl you don't know the half of it!" I continued. I proceeded to tell Diamond all about the raid at the club and how Duke picked me up. I told her about our fucking session. I knew her so well I could tell Diamond was on the edge of her seat listening to me. I know you don't supposed to tell other women, even friends, about lovemaking sessions with your men, but I really did trust Diamond with my life. Then I dropped the bomb on her. "And girl, he gave me the keys to this hot ass condo and told me to move in!" I announced loudly. All of a sudden the line went quiet.

"Did you hear me, Dee! He gave me a damn condo in the Cosmo building!" I screamed again.

"Yeah, I heard you," she replied weakly. "Girl, that is so good for you. I guess that means I'll be looking for a new roommate, huh?" I could hear the sadness in her voice.

Shit! I hadn't really thought about Diamond being left in the apartment by herself, without my half of the rent. "Well, since Duke isn't making me pay anything, I will still help you pay the rent for awhile until you can find somebody to take my room," I offered, feeling kind of guilty that I was leaving her.

"You sure this is what you wanna do, Nini?" Diamond asked.

"Hell yeah, Diamond!" I answered her excitedly, leaving no doubt what I thought. "Shit, what if Brian came and offered you keys to a brand new, fully furnished condo and told you that you didn't have to pay shit? Let's be real, you would be gone so fast I would be seeing smoke behind you."

"I guess you're right," Diamond said in a low tone. "I mean, this is what we both wanted for ourselves . . . a good man with money to take care of us. Just be careful and don't fall too hard for that nigga. I heard Duke Carrington is known around Virginia Beach as a big time ladies man."

I didn't believe this shit. Not Diamond, but then again, why not Diamond. To me she sounded like she was hating on me again. I couldn't understand it at all and it annoyed the hell out of me. She was my BFF, but the hatorade was killing me.

"Well Diamond, you were the one telling me to get with him . . . so why the change of heart now?" I snapped at her. Diamond was quiet for a few seconds and then she came back at me.

"I only wanted you to go out with him and get him to pay a few of our bills," she stated. "I wasn't advocating for you to move into his place with him and fall all in love. But do what you want, I'm just saying to be careful because once you give a nigga your all and he doesn't give you his ain't no turning back then."

I was getting madder by the minute so I wanted to cut our conversation short before me and my best friend had yet another falling out. "Trust me, I have everything under control, my feelings for Duke included," I retorted.

"A'ight, I warned you."

"I'm going shopping with the stack of cash Duke left me and then I'll be by to pick up some of my stuff. Like I said, it's probably best that you start looking for another roommate!" I snapped back. Diamond was quiet. "Hello?" I said into the receiver.

"Good luck, Lynise . . . that's all I can wish you dealing with that dude," she said spitefully.

"Diamond, let me go. Like I said, I'm a grown ass woman and I am dealing with a real man. I got this under control. I will be dropping off my keys today. Talk to you later." Then I cut the call off.

I wasn't going to entertain Diamond's ill-feelings or ill-thoughts. I told myself she was hating on my new man and my soon-to-be lavish living. She chose Brian and I was sorry her life sucked. But I was glad she had convinced me to give Duke a chance. It had to be all uphill from here. *From my viewpoint, life could only get better.*

Chapter 9
I Know What Girls Like

I took a cab to the club and picked up my car. I looked at my little beat down ride and knew that the first thing I was going to get me when I moved up to wifey status with Duke was going to be a new car. I drove to my old apartment and was kind of praying that Diamond wasn't there. I didn't want to see her just in case she started acting all stank and looking sad and shit when I took my stuff.

I went inside the apartment and took arms full of clothes and shoes. There was nothing I had as exclusive and expensive as what Duke had bought me so I grabbed that shit first. It took me several trips and my little car was packed with my stuff. I decided to go to the mall to buy me some sexy lingerie and maybe some hot shoes with the money Duke gave me.

I couldn't have been happier. I raced around the upscale mall like I owned it. I picked up La Perla underwear and lingerie. Then I tried on almost twenty pairs of Brian Atwood,

Christian Louboutin and Giuseppe Zanotti shoes. I finally settled on another pair of Louboutins. There was just something about those shoes that said sexy and sophisticated. It felt so good to go to the register, ring up my shit and pay with cash. It also felt good getting the little arched eyebrow surprised looks from the salesclerks inside the store. I wanted to just scream out "Yeah bitches, I can afford it because my man provides!" I didn't though. I was quiet and I held my head high like a sophisticated lady would. In my mind, I wouldn't have to pretend to be a sophisticated lady because I was on my way to claim that title.

I literally shopped until I felt ready to drop. After a while, I drove back to the condo and started the tedious task of unloading my new and old shit into the condo. It took me at least twenty trips with arms full of stuff to finish unpacking my things. Initially, I put everything in the living room. When I had everything inside, I flopped on the couch, put my feet up and rested for a minute. I looked around again at the condo and its beautiful furnishing and couldn't believe it was all mine now. "Ewwwweeee!" I sang and kicked my feet in a joyous display. "Calm down, Lynise!" I called out to myself and then started laughing. I was fucking delirious with joy.

I looked at the clock on the cable box and saw that it was getting late. I decided to start putting my stuff away so Duke wouldn't come home to find a big mess. I didn't want my new *boo* to think I was a dirty bitch.

I carried the new bags of stuff into the bedroom, put them down and pulled back the doors to the walk-in closet. That shit was almost completely empty, which meant it was all mine. Duke had a few custom-made dress shirts hanging up inside but not much else. "Perfect!" I said excitedly. I dragged the bags inside and started unloading my new shoes first. There were shoe drawers with clear fronts built into the closet. I would never have to open a million shoe boxes looking for a certain pair of shoes anymore. Nor would I have to worry about keeping a ton of shoe boxes.

"This is really high post," I said to myself. I unloaded the new things and then I started putting some of my old things from the apartment inside the closet. I made several trips back and forth between the bedroom and living room before I heard the front door rattling. My heart jumped in my chest. It was Duke! I instantly grew excited to see him. I raced into the closet and kept putting things inside acting like I didn't hear him. I didn't want him to think I was dying to see him . . . even though I was.

"Beautiful!" he called out to me. I smiled as I listened to his voice grow closer and closer. "Oh, there you are. Damn, you ain't wasting no time, huh?" Duke walked into the closet and grabbed me around my waist. He pulled me close to him and I turned around to give him a kiss.

"Naw, none of that nice, nice shit right now. I have been thinking about this pussy all day. I couldn't even concentrate at my meeting," Duke huffed. Then he spun me around roughly. I let out a short whimper. He hoisted up the mini skirt I had on and ripped my thongs off.

"Oww!" I yelped as the thong's material kind of dug into my skin.

"Put your hands on that shelf," Duke wolfed. I did as he asked. He pushed down on my back and bent me over. Then he bent down and licked from my pussy to my ass to get my shit wet.

"Ahh," I let out a sigh. That shit felt so good. Duke let a glob of spit fall between my ass and he used his thumb to swipe it up and down my pussy. "Yes," I whispered.

Duke put his strong hand on my shoulder for leverage and then he drove his thick, stiff, dick into my pussy with force.

"Owww!" I screamed. That shit hurt so good. Duke immediately started pounding me from the back. For a minute I thought he was going to send me through the closet wall.

I grasped the shelf to make sure he didn't bang my head through the wall. I was yelping and screaming as Duke tore my pussy up. He slapped my ass and fucked the living shit out of me. My pussy throbbed and my ass cheeks were stinging.

"Yes daddy! Fuck me Daddy!" I screamed out. I knew how to get Duke right to the point of no return.

"Shhh! You know that shit drives me wild," he grunted. But it was too late. "Ughhh!" he strained as he pushed real deep into my pussy. He was coming and I knew it.

Again, this nigga didn't wear a condom. At that point, I was too deep in ecstasy to even care. I felt Duke's dick get limp and slip out of my pussy. Some of his cum dripped onto my legs. He pulled up his pants and took a deep breath.

"Was that good to you?" I asked in a seductive tone.

"What? You asking a stupid question. You got some good ass pussy girl."

I couldn't stop smiling. "Good. All I wanna do is please you," I replied. I couldn't believe I had started falling in love with Duke so fast. But the feeling I had in my gut told me I was definitely falling.

I followed Duke out of the closet and noticed he was cleaning himself up. I looked at him strangely. I thought he was home for the night.

"Where you going?" I said, putting on a sad baby face.

Duke laughed like I said something funny. "Beautiful, I'm going home. I said you could live here, but I'm not living here," he surprisingly informed me. "I'll be back of course, because I can't resist that pussy. I told you already . . . I live all over the place."

It was kind of a shocker because I had just assumed once he asked me to live in the condo we would be living together like a couple. I guess I was wrong. But I didn't complain. I let a fake smile spread across my face anyway.

"But look, here is a lil' something to keep you busy while I'm busy," Duke said, pulling out a wad of cash from his pocket.

"You already gave me money," I gasped looking at the money.

"And as long as you're good, I'll keep giving you money," Duke said, kissing me and placing the clean, crisp bills in my hand.

I didn't want to act too hype and count them in front of him. I just held them tightly. "Thank you for everything," I said meaningfully.

"Just stay sweet," Duke said and then he headed out of the bedroom towards the door.

"Will you call or come over tomorrow!" I called after him. I was feeling a little anxious that he was leaving.

"Just be available whenever I do call," Duke answered back.

My shoulders slumped at that answer. When I was sure I was alone I ran over to the bed and spread the cash out. Duke had given me thirty one hundred dollar bills. "Three thousand dollars!" I screamed out loud happy as shit. I lifted the money and threw some in the air and then I laid in the rest and rolled around like a pig in slop. This was a lifestyle I could surely get used to. I had never had a man who came anywhere close to Duke.

He was definitely a keeper!

CHAPTER 10
MONEY HUNGRY

It had been a few days since Duke had come to the condo and I was starting to get stir crazy.

I called Diamond and we met up to spend some of Duke's money. I should say *my money*. Diamond looked kind of skinny to me. I was sure it was the unneeded stress from her man, Brian. If I loved a fool like that I'm sure I would be stressed the hell out as well.

We went to the Gucci store and I got her a bag. I figured there would be more money coming my way and Diamond was still struggling and shaking her ass at the club, so why not. After all, she was still my girl and I was sure she would do the same for me.

Next, we went to lunch on me. It felt good being with her again. When we parted ways, we hugged. As I drove to the condo, I was secretly hoping Duke would be there.

Sure enough, when I turned the key to the condo door I didn't hear the alarm beep. I instantly got excited because that meant that Duke had punched in the code already. I began to call out to him but then I heard voices. I crinkled my eyebrows and listened for a minute. It was Duke and another man's voice. It was coming from the den. I tiptoed near the den's door and listened for a minute. I didn't want to interrupt any important meetings. I peeked around the doorway a little bit. Duke and an older gentleman were standing by the big windows. They both had their backs to me, so I ducked back out of the door and listened.

"Dr. Gavin, I'm trusting you to totally run this shit. I've sunken a lot of money into this," Duke said.

"Yes, yes, Mr. Carrington. Here are the photos of the girls I promised you," the man called Dr. Gavin stated. He looked to be in his fifties, but I only saw him from behind. He handed Duke a stack of photos. I was real interested now that I'd heard him say *girls*.

"Shit, they look good to be big and pregnant. I guess young chicks keep their bodies when they get pregnant," Duke commented as he flipped through the photos.

Pregnant! Young girls! I screamed inside of my head. What the fuck was Duke into? Now I had to listen. It was as if my feet were stuck. I quietly slipped my shoes off just to make sure they didn't hear me.

"Where's the newest one you were telling me about?" Duke asked. "You know, the one you said looked mixed and may have a white looking baby."

"She's right here," Dr. Gavin said, pulling a picture from the stack and putting it on top. "This girl is eighteen years old and she's homeless. She came to the Help Center to get shelter but she doesn't want to give up her baby for adoption," Dr. Gavin informed Duke.

"Well then you know what to do with the bitch! I don't want to hear no fucking excuses. I got a lot of money on the line and a lot of fucking people have paid me a lot of fucking money so if you don't do the right thing, then I'm going to find someone else who will," Duke snapped at the doctor.

The old man looked frightened to death. "Yes, Mr. Carrington. I know what to do. They all trust me to deliver their babies, so it would be no problem for me to sedate them and make the babies disappear."

Oh Shit! I placed my hands over my lips. They sounded as if they were about to wrap up their meeting, so I started quickly tiptoeing back to the door. My heart was hammering from the shit I had just heard. It sounded as if Duke was into some black market baby snatching type of illegal adoption shit. He had actually hired a fucking doctor to snatch young girls' babies.

My legs were kind of weak as I tipped away. I was finally at the front door and I snuck back out. I stood outside the door for a few minutes with my chest rising and falling rapidly. "Pull it together, Lynise. His business has nothing to do with you," I told myself. I decided to put what I had heard out of my mind. *Why should I give up my lavish living to save young bitches?* I reasoned.

I put the key back in the door as if I had just made it home. I opened the door and called out. "Duke? Are you here?" I called out, faking like a muthfucka. "Baby? I'm home!" I sang out. I started towards the den. I got to the door just in time to see Duke scrambling to put the fucking pictures and paperwork in his brief case.

"Oh, I didn't know you had company," I lied.

"Wassup, Beautiful. Did you have a good day?" Duke said nervously. Then he looked over at the doctor.

"Dr. Gavin, this is my new wifey, Lynise. Lynise, this is my business associate, Dr. Gavin," Duke introduced us. I put on a real fake smile and extended my hand for a shake. However, instead of shaking my hand, the doctor grabbed it and planted a wet kiss on the top of my hand. That shit made me cringe. Especially since I knew what kind of fucking monster he was.

"It is very nice to meet you," the creepy doctor said.

"Same here," I lied.

"Mr. Carrington, I will be in touch," Dr. Gavin said and with that the creepy doctor departed the condo.

Duke came over to me and as usual he wanted to place his long tongue down my throat. Any other day I had welcomed his deep, choking kisses. But after what I had heard I was kind of turned off. I kissed him back but not with the same fever as before.

"You alright, Beautiful?" Duke asked me.

"Oh, I'm fine. Can we hang out and get it on?" I faked a smile.

"Naw, I gotta go again," Duke said. "But I promise to see you either tomorrow or in a few days." I felt a pang of disappointment. "But the good news is I have something for you."

I perked right up. That always worked. Duke dug in his pocket while I waited with baited breath. I assumed he would pull out some more cash, which would've been fine with me. Imagine my fucking surprise when Duke pulled out the keys to a brand new BMW X-6.

"Beautiful, these are yours. You can't live in this condo driving that piece of shit you got," he announced. I started jumping up and down. Duke led me to the balcony in the bedroom, which had a view of the front of the building and the parking lot. "There she is, the candy apple red one," Duke pointed out my new car.

"Oh, thank you baby!" I screamed, hugging him around his neck as tight as I could.

"No problem. Just always be good. I gotta go now."

I let him go. Hell, I was too excited about the car to be disappointed about him leaving. I guess living with what I knew about his business dealings with the doctor had just gotten a lot easier.

Chapter 11
Money, Hoes & Clothes

When Duke left I raced downstairs and got into my new whip.

I really loved everything about it. I took it for a spin around the neighborhood and I tried to use the new car as a distraction to clear my mind from what I had heard earlier. It absolutely didn't work. To think of my sweet man being involved in something that might hurt young girls or their babies left me feeling kind of sick. I wasn't that trifling or shallow that a car or a million pairs of shoes could change how I felt.

After playing Duke's conversation with Dr. Gavin repeatedly in my mind, I started doubting myself. I returned to the condo and tried to watch television. That shit didn't work either. So I tried to play fashion show and tried on several of the clothes I had purchased over the past few weeks. Shit like that usually made me happy, but once again I struck out. I paced the condo before finally deciding to check out the den to see if Duke had left any evidence behind. Nothing.

My mind raced with all kinds of thoughts. "Sounded like an illegal baby snatching ring," I stated aloud as I stood in the middle of the living room with my hands on my hips. "Arrgghh!" I screamed in frustration.

I had to stop driving myself crazy. Duke was nothing but a fucking gentleman and a businessman I told myself. I wanted to believe that I had not heard right. I needed somebody to take my mind off this shit. You guessed it, I called Diamond. After all, she was still my BFF.

"Diamond!" I yelled into the phone. I sounded as if I would just bust out crying. Of course this alarmed her because we had just had a damn blast shopping. After she asked me what was wrong I went right into it.

"Diamond, oh my God, you're not going to believe this!" I said with urgency. She screamed in my ear telling me to get to the damn point. "I think Duke is into an illegal adoption and baby snatching ring!" I blurted out.

Diamond got kind of quiet.

"Did you hear me?!" I asked her. I was confused as to why she wasn't asking me for details. So I just started telling her. "I crept in on him having a conversation with a man named Dr. Gavin. That old bastard was showing Duke pictures of young pregnant chicks and Duke told him if they didn't want to give up their babies that the doctor should just take them because he had a lot of money out there riding on this." I relayed verbatim what I'd heard. I wanted Diamond to feel the effect of what I had overheard.

But Diamond was sullen and quiet until she told me she had something to tell me. Then she indeed dropped the bomb on my ass. She had already heard that Duke was in the illegal adoption business. Evidently Dr. Gavin was the front man who ran a homeless shelter in Chesapeake for pregnant women who were abused or raped. If the women didn't want to give up their babies willingly, then Dr. Gavin would deliver the babies by C-section while the mother was knocked out. When the women awakened, Dr. Gavin would tell them their babies died at birth.

I gripped my cell to my ear in disbelief at what I was hearing. I had never held a phone so tightly. "Diamond, why didn't you tell me this shit before now!" I screamed at her. Tears were running down my face. I didn't want to believe my knight in shining armor was really a fucking grim reaper.

Diamond didn't tell me because I was too caught up and so in love with Duke. She didn't want me to accuse her of trying to break us up or hating on our relationship.

Hell, she was right.

Had I not heard it for myself and if Diamond had tried to tell me anything bad about Duke, I would've accused her of wanting him and being jealous that I had a good man.

"What am I going to do now. If I move out he might be asking questions. I can't let him know that I know anything," I told her.

Diamond told me to sit tight and just enjoy the money and gifts. She told me not to worry about his business. She also warned me to be very careful because she had also heard that Duke could be a very violent and dangerous man.

That part didn't sit right with me. Duke was definitely a businessman and maybe this whole baby shit was just a misunderstanding, but he was far from dangerous. "I don't think he would hurt me Diamond. You have to see how good he treats me when we're together. He has told me a billion times how much he loves my sex," I reported to her.

Diamond wasn't trying to hear it. She wasn't convinced Duke wouldn't hurt me. She told me if his business or money was compromised he might just kill his own mother.

I laughed and scoffed at Diamond's paranoia. I kindly dismissed her warning and assured her again that Duke wouldn't hurt me. "Girl, I got that man eating out the palm of my hands" I said.

But no matter what I said, Diamond wasn't convinced at all.

CHAPTER 12
IS THAT YO' BITCH?

Before Diamond and I ended our conversation I agreed to meet her at the *Magic City* for a drink and just to hang out.

I hadn't been to the club in days and I knew Neeko had probably fired me. I didn't care. For now, that wasn't my life anymore. I had a lot on my mind and I needed a drink and I also needed a hug from my BFF.

I drove my new whip to the club. When I pulled into the parking lot, Diamond was standing outside puffing on a cigarette and talking to the club's DJ. She turned around for a minute but didn't realize it was me driving the car. She took a drag off her cigarette and went back to her conversation. That is, until she saw me stepping out of the BMW. I saw the DJ motion towards me and Diamond turned back around. Her eyes grew as wide as dinner plates, she flicked her cigarette to the ground and started screaming.

"Ahhhh! Oh no he didn't, bitch! Oh my God! Nini! He bought that ass a fucking X6!

Her excited ass raced over to me and snatched the keys out of my hand. "Bitch, you know I gotta test drive this shit!" her face lighting up like a kid at Christmas.

I was laughing. She had already taken my mind off the issue with Duke.

"Come the fuck on! I might never get another chance to drive a fucking beamer!" Diamond urged as she pulled my arm.

We jumped back in my new car and Diamond peeled out of the club's parking lot. "Slow down bitch, I just got it!" I said jokingly.

"Oh my God, this fucking whip is so hot! I am so feeling it, Lynise!" Diamond complimented. I felt really good that she approved. We drove around while she continued screaming and acted overly excited. "Lynise, you better not leave that nigga over no fucking baby snatching bullshit. Look, them bitches' babies are probably better off wherever he is selling them at."

I couldn't believe the shit out of Diamond's mouth as she whipped my ride down the highway. "Oh my goodness, Diamond, I cannot believe you're saying this shit because he bought me a car!" I yelled at her. "You was just telling me to be careful this and careful that . . . the nigga is dangerous, you said! Now you changing your damn tune?" I made my point as I smiled at how quickly a luxury whip had persuaded her that Duke was now a good guy.

"Um . . . bitch! He bought you a car, gave you a condo and fucking enough cash for you to take me shopping with you!" she stated. "Ok, I'm thinking your ass need to be the fuck quiet and just ride! As long as you stay quiet and play your position my warnings won't be needed."

I shook my head at my girl. I was just amazed at the excitement in her voice. I actually think she had forgotten that fast the shit she was telling me about Duke.

"I'm not going to say anything to him right now, but I still want you to remember that you were the one telling me the nigga might kill me or some shit," I informed her.

"Girl, fuck all that," Diamond said with a hint of laughter in her voice. "Get what you can and make sure you stash in the process. Shit, if it was me I would have a nigga so sewn up that he wouldn't know what to do and if that muthafucka ever tried to play me, I promise to show his ass that that old fucking saying, *it's cheaper to keep her . . .* is the truth."

Even with the laughter, I knew her ass was dead serious though.

We pulled back into the club's parking lot. After hanging and cruising with Diamond for those few minutes I was already feeling better. I started having second thoughts about going into the club now. I mean, I did just up and walk out on my damn job.

"C'mon girl. I'ma make sure I tell Neeko about your new ride. Let that greasy, jheri curl wearing asshole know you don't need to be slanging no damn drinks for his grungy ass customers," Diamond said.

Although I had plans to return to the condo after our short cruise, hearing her level of excitement made me want to stick around longer. So I decided to go inside and have a quick drink with Diamond. Besides, I knew Duke probably wouldn't be coming back to the condo tonight. He hardly ever stayed the entire night with me.

Once inside, I noticed the club was already packed. The second thing I noticed was the clientele had changed. I saw less of the higher paying patrons and more of the losers that came in there to try to get cheap sex. I noticed some of the broke niggas I knew by name peppered throughout the smoky club. Both Diamond and I climbed up on barstools. It felt funny being on the other side of the bar.

Diamond tapped on the bar top and the girl I usually competed with for tips, Raven, came over to take our drink orders. She looked surprised to see me and twisted up her lips. I rolled my eyes and placed my newly purchased Gucci bag on top of the bar in Raven's face. She took our orders and stomped away. I just laughed.

"Girl, you better go get dressed for your set," I told Diamond.

"Fuck Neeko. When I'm ready I will get ready. Besides, I'm having a drink with my new rich friend!" Diamond said jokingly, slapping my thigh.

"That is not funny girl," I replied. "I am very far from rich. Let's get it right. I don't have shit . . . he has all the money."

Raven slammed our drinks down in front of us. I had ordered a Pink Lady and Diamond ordered a Mojito. "What the fuck is wrong with that ugly bitch?" Diamond asked in response to Raven's very apparent attitude.

"I guess she didn't ever expect me to be buying a drink instead of serving one."

As we bullshitted at the bar and talked about everybody in the club, a dude approached and stood between us. That shit was rude to begin with. I looked at him with my face curled into a frown. He was a very dark skinned, short, big bellied, troll in my eyes. Diamond lifted her drink and rolled her eyes as if she knew who he was. I had never seen him before. I started talking over him. I wasn't going to acknowledge his rude ass at all.

"I'm saying can I get with you?" the little, charcoal colored stranger said to me. I turned around to look behind me to see if he was speaking to someone else and then looked back at him as if he was crazy. I just knew he couldn't be talking to me.

"What?" I snapped, disgust very apparent on my upturned face.

"I'll give you a'hunned dollars for a champagne room dick suck," he said with a nasty, perverted tone to his voice. Then he licked his ashy lips. I didn't think I was hearing his ass correctly.

"What did you say?" I retorted.

"You heard me . . . I wanna get my dick sucked and I want you to do it," the troll said, grabbing a handful of his own crotch. I could've thrown up on him at just the thought.

"Muthfucka, get outta my face! I ain't no fucking ho'! Ya dick probably ain't even big enough to be sucked anyway! Get the fuck on!" I screamed at his ass.

"What bitch? Fuck you! You ain't all that!" the man barked, getting closer to me as if he was going to lay hands on me or something. I jumped off the stool and stood toe-to-toe with him. I didn't want to be sitting down just in case he tried to get slap happy. I was on my defensive. Diamond jumped up too. But I didn't even give her a chance to say anything.

"Get the fuck out of my face you dirty, little dick piece of shit!" I cursed right in the loser's face.

"Ya friend wasn't saying that shit when my big dick was down her throat last night!" he spat cruelly. I shot Diamond a look. "Excuse me for thinking hoes of a feather, flock together!" the man continued.

Diamond looked as if she wanted to just run away. Before I even thought about it I threw my drink in his face.

Then I threw the glass at him. It bounced off his jelly belly and crashed to the floor.

"You fucking bitch! I will fucking kill you!" he screamed and then he lurched towards me.

Before he could put his hands on me I heard a loud crack and all of a sudden the ugly stranger crumpled to the floor. He was holding his head and screaming. My eyes grew wide. I looked to my left and Duke was standing there shaking his hand. His knuckles were bleeding from hitting the asshole.

The guy scrambled up off the floor. "Oh, is that yo' bitch? This ain't the end of this shit!" he screamed at Duke.

"No bitch ass nigga, that's my woman," Duke said in a scary calm voice. "You know, something you'll never have. Now nigga, you better go 'head. I'm not one of these average cats up in here." By then the club's security had their hands on the dude and was carrying his ass towards the door. He was still screaming obscenities about what he was going to do the next time he saw me or Duke.

My eyes were wide and I had my hand over my mouth. I don't know if I was more shocked to see Duke there or that he had hit the guy to defend me.

"So Beautiful, whatcha doing up in here?" Duke asked me. He seemed a little annoyed with me being there. I opened my mouth but no words came out. "I told you that you needed to quit this job. I thought I hit you off with enough dough and shit that you knew you didn't have to be up in this shithole trying to work no bar," Duke chastised.

I couldn't even explain to him that I was only there to spend time with Diamond. Duke grabbed my arm kind of forcefully and told me we were leaving. "See you later girl," I said to Diamond. She didn't even respond. Duke and I left the club together.

"You didn't have to basically snatch me up outta the club, Duke," I complained. "I could've just walked out if you would've said let's go home."

He walked me to my car. When I was about to get in he finally spoke.

"From now on when I tell you something . . . listen. I think I know best right now," Duke said sternly.

Was he kidding me? He sounded like a father, not like a brand new ass boyfriend.

"I wasn't there to work! But you never said you were going to provide for my every need either, so if I was there to work it's because I'm not even sure about us Duke! I have been at the condo for days and I only see you for minutes," I shot back.

"Well, I'm gonna provide you what you need! No woman of mine needs to be working in a shithole where niggas gonna be disrespecting you," he said firmly. "If you wanna see your little girlfriend tell her to come by the condo or meet you at the mall. But you are not to come back to this place."

I felt all mushy inside when he said that. I thought it was so cute that he was putting his foot down to take care of me. He was demanding that I not return to the club . . . how manly was that. I loved that man and I knew it for sure now. Only real men stepped up and told a chick she didn't have to work. I had been waiting all my life for a man like Duke Carrington to come along. *Finally!* I said in my mind as I pulled my car out of the parking lot.

"A man that wants to act like a damn real man. I can definitely dig that," I mumbled out loud with my new car smell wafting in my nostrils.

Duke and I went our separate ways in separate cars. It wasn't until I returned to the empty condo that I remembered something . . . I had forgotten to ask Duke what the hell he was doing up in the strip club himself.

CHAPTER 13
MO' PROBLEMS

Six Months Earlier.

Once again, I woke up to an empty bed.

I rolled over and looked at Duke's side of the bed, still neatly made up, not even an indentation in his pillow. I sighed loudly and looked over at the clock. I closed my eyes in disgust. I couldn't even get used to sleeping late anymore. It was six in the morning and I was up with no place to go and nothing to do except wait on Duke to come hit me off with some money or another guilt gift. That's what our relationship had become. He was becoming more and more scarce around the condo, so I had come to expect those *sorry I fucked up* gifts every time I saw him now. His routine was so predictable now. He'd disappear for days, one time even an entire week, then he would come to the condo with some expensive gift, a long story and his dick and I'd be his again.

It was so bad I gave Diamond some of the *make up* gifts. Sometimes he would buy the same gift in a different color because he couldn't remember what he had purchased last. That was a damn shame. If I had two or three of the same item I would give Diamond one. So far she had acquired two David Yurman ring and bracelet sets, a fur stole, numerous bags from various premier designers and a bunch of diamond jewelry.

I picked up my cell and there was not even one missed call from Duke. He had come two nights prior and he seemed to be in a crazy rush. He had disappeared into the den and locked the door, which was strange. Initially when he put the fucking door on the den I had become suspicious, but I never ventured in that room. The last night he was here, I was so glad to see him I didn't even question his apparent urgency to get in and out.

But laying in the bed with nothing to do, lonely and bored, I started to think about how frantic Duke seemed to be. Even his sex was different that night. That fact alone made me very curious about what the fuck he had going on. I got up and pulled myself together, brushed my teeth and got the sleep cobwebs out of my head. Then I wrapped a silk robe around my body and shuffled my feet to the den door. I jiggled with the knob and the door popped open. I didn't have shit else to do so I decided to snoop. It was something I had never had the urge to do until now. Duke hadn't given me any real reason to suspect him of anything other than maybe his shady business with Dr. Gavin. I mean, shit had been great between us for a while.

After Duke made me quit the job at the club, he was very attentive to me for a good long minute. We spent our nights going to dinner at exclusive places and having wild uninhibited sex, and I spent my days spending Duke's money at various malls and boutiques. I had taken several trips to New York to shop at some of the swanky, one-of-a-kind boutiques in SoHo. I can't front, I was living the good life. Duke had even sent me on an all expense paid trip to Turks and Caicos Islands. I had offered to take Diamond but she wouldn't dare leave Virginia Beach without that piece of shit man she was still carrying.

I lived each day as if shit was all good and I didn't have time to complain. So snooping into Duke's business wasn't high on my list of priorities. I had long since put what I had learned about him to the far ends of my mind. I just wanted to enjoy the shit he was providing. I wanted to work my way to being his wife, so I kept my mouth shut and my legs wide open. But six months after I had given up everything for Duke, I found myself alone and wondering what the fuck was keeping him away from me all the time. I told myself that my burning desire to know was human nature. Curiosity killed the cat, but is also a natural part of life. Anybody would've gotten nosey by now, especially a woman bored as hell.

I walked into the den and looked around. Nothing looked amiss. Well, it wouldn't have since Duke paid a cleaning lady to come into the condo every other week. I didn't even have to clean, that's how deep this shit was. I walked over to Duke's desk. Of course, all of the drawers were locked. "Shit!" I cursed, disappointed. I flopped down in his leather swivel chair and turned it towards the big window. Looking out towards the beach, the view from the condo was simply breathtaking. But it caused me to shake my head. I didn't have my man there to enjoy the beach with me.

"Fuck this bullshit," I grumbled. I was mad, somewhat pissed off. This wasn't what I envisioned. I jumped out of the chair and raced into the kitchen. I opened all of the counter drawers looking for a knife. It was a damn shame I didn't even know where the knives were, because I had never had to cook a meal in the condo.

"Finally!" I gasped as I located a steak knife. With my heart racing, I rushed back to the den. I immediately started jimmying the locks. My hands were shaking which was making it nearly impossible for me to get the damn locks popped. "Dammit!" I cursed, pushing my hair out of my face. I was exasperated. I stood up and looked around.

"Where would somebody with a billion places to live leave the keys?" I verbally asked myself. I stopped and tried to focus, get my thoughts together. And that's when it hit me, I was thinking like me and not like Duke. That's what I needed to do, think like Duke Carrington.

I knew the keys were there in the house. Then it came to me as if it was a vision from God. Every time Duke came to the condo he went straight into our closet and then he would go into the den, put away whatever he had to put up and then come to me.

"So fucking predictable," I growled as I rushed back to the bedroom. First, I opened the nightstand drawers on his side of the bed. Duke had opened the drawers several times during his visits to the condo. The drawers were empty. I went into our closet and rifled through the pockets of the three pairs of pants he left at the condo. Another dead end . . . I didn't find anything.

My shoulders slumped in disappointment. Then I spotted the black Armani blazer hanging all by its lonesome a few feet away from the pants. My heart skipped a beat because I knew I was on point with the blazer. I raced over to the blazer and dug in the outside pockets. Shit, nothing. Then, I reached into the inside, breast pocket.

"A-fuckin'-ha! Bingo!" I screamed, as my hands shook uncontrollably. There was a set of keys in the blazer's inside pocket. My mouth was as dry as the scorching desert as I gulped a lump of fear. I don't know why I was so scared, because I was alone and the alarm was on so if Duke tried to come in I would definitely hear him. I gripped the keys tightly for a minute. I was hesitating.

This sucked. I had racked my brain looking for these fucking keys and now that I had found them, I was hesitant to use them. "Lynise put the keys back," I whispered to myself. No! I was going to open that damn desk. I had to open those desk drawers. I ran through the condo as if someone was chasing me. When I reached the den, I fumbled with the keys. The first key didn't work. Then the second key didn't work. It was the fourth key that finally opened the drawers on the desk. I bent down and pulled open the first drawer. Inside was just a little composition notebook. I opened it and read some of the pages. I placed my hand over my lips.

There were names of clients . . . damn, there were definitely names. Names of the rich ones who wanted to buy babies on the black market. There were also money amounts next to the names.

"What the fuck," I gasped when I saw an amount as high as two million dollars scribbled in Duke's handwriting next to the name Barkers. I dropped the book back into the drawer like it was a poisonous snake ready to fill me up with venom. Then I opened the big drawer on the bottom. I found a black lock box. The kind storeowners used to transport their cash to banks after a profitable night. I quickly found out the box was locked as well. I picked the keys up and immediately noticed the round safe key. I slowly and deliberately inserted the key into the lock box.

My eyes grew wide when I looked inside. There were about ten stacks of money bonded together with thick black rubber bands. Underneath the money were T-Bills—some as large as five thousand dollars. I couldn't understand why Duke had money in that box. Then I noticed a folded up piece of paper. I unfolded it and read it.

Wine and Dine Cash. Lynise. Dana. Audrey. Amber. Lisette.

I threw the paper down, back into the box. My head was spinning. I immediately felt sick to my stomach. *What the fuck he means wine and dine cash? Why the fuck are there so many bitches' names on this fucking list!* I was ready to explode. My mind was in overdrive. I didn't know what the fuck to do. In a blind rage, I reached down into the box and grabbed two stacks of money. I took a stack of bills right out of the middle and set the money on the desk. They were all one hundred dollar bills.

"Muthafucka!" I managed through my newly formed tears. I quickly locked the box back up and put it back into the drawer. I went through the drawers on the other side of the desk. In those I found paperwork related to Duke's businesses, utility bills and his other homes. I took a bunch of stuff with me. I was going to keep everything, including the money. I had to find a safe place to keep everything. My investigative thinking cap was on now. I was starting to have a good fucking idea of why my so-called *perfect man* was disappearing so much. I understood the *disappearing acts* now. It was on.

I dried my tears. Got my composure—refocused.

Then I went and made myself of copy of all those fucking keys too.

Duke didn't know who he was fucking with!

CHAPTER 14

FAKING JACKS

It was three days after my discovery of the money and list of chicks when Duke finally made an appearance at the condo.

It was the middle of the night when I heard him punching in the alarm code. I bit into my bottom lip and tried my best to put on the *I love you so much* act. I could hear Duke shuffling around inside the closet. Then he went to the den. That shit made me squeeze the pillow, I was so angry. All I could think of was that he was adding more bitches' names to his list.

Duke undressed and slid into bed. He cuddled behind me and started kissing my ears. I just moved a little bit. Usually, I just rolled over and welcomed him. Not tonight. Duke started licking my neck and letting his hands roam all over my body. I stiffened because my mind started wondering if he had been with another woman . . . any of those bitches I saw on his list. Duke touched my breasts and pinched my nipples. That shit made me feel kind of dirty. Then he pulled me onto my back.

"Wassup with you, baby? You ain't happy to see your man?" he said in a supposedly low sexy tone. His breath was hot and smelled of alcohol. A pang of jealousy shot through me. I wanted to ask him who the fuck he was out wining and dining with tonight. But I remained silent.

Duke proceeded to take what he wanted. Eventually he was able to get between my rigid, stiff legs. I pumped up and down, and didn't even bother to fuck him back like I usually did. I know he noticed too, because he kept stopping and looking at me strangely. Whenever he did that I called out, "yeah baby, oh baby," in my most fake voice. Duke wasn't stupid, I'm sure he knew something was up. He started fucking me real hard and I was having minor sharp pains in my abdomen. I also noticed my breasts were super sore and sensitive when he sucked them. I was glad as hell when he finally came.

He rolled off of me and I turned my back. Again, not my usual self. I would usually rub and caress him after sex. Cuddle up, lay my head and upper body on his chest and talk to him. Tonight I wasn't up for that shit.

Duke didn't sweat it either. He just turned over and went to sleep. I couldn't get back to sleep, not with all the shit I had on my mind. And to top it all off, this nigga had actually showed up this time without even bothering to buy me a guilt gift. He was really slacking now. It was all good because I knew he had put more money in that fucking box and I was intending to take my share. I had finally heeded Diamond's words . . . I was stashing little by little just in case some shit ever jumped off. I wasn't going to be like those rich men's wives that sat around thinking their shit didn't stink and never having a Plan B. I had already started putting my Plan B in place . . . *just in case.*

Duke got up the next morning and he didn't say much to me at first. I stayed in bed while he showered and got ready to leave, once again. I was feeling sick to my stomach. I didn't know if it was the anxiety of him leaving me again, coupled with the fact that I didn't know when he'd be coming back, or if I was coming down with something. I felt like throwing up and I had the worst headache.

"Baby, something wrong?" Duke asked when he emerged from the bathroom and started putting on his clothes.

"I'm just lonely and I miss you when you stay away so long. Why don't you want to spend time with me anymore?" I said somberly.

Duke had a stoic look on his face. "What . . . all this I'm giving you ain't enough?" he asked evilly. I was shocked by his nasty reaction to my question. He was definitely not the same man I met and thought was the shit. Now his shit was stinking up the place.

"I'm not saying that but—" I started to say but was rudely interrupted.

"But nothing! I'm saying if you ain't happy here you can leave," Duke blasted back.

"Why are you being so mean!?" I screamed. Unable to control my emotions, I suddenly burst out crying.

Duke chuckled. "You young girls gotta get it together. You knew I was busy when I picked your ass up out the gutter," Duke said maliciously. Then he walked out of the bedroom. He left me crying hysterically.

"Ahhhhh!" I screamed out of frustration when I heard the condo door slam. I was beside myself. I laid back down and cried until my chest hurt.

When I finally pulled myself together, I noticed that Duke had left me a stack of cash on the dining room table. I picked it up and flipped through it. It was his usual $3,000.

"I will just go shopping and make myself feel better," I mumbled. I knew damn well buying even more clothes than I had already acquired over the past six months wasn't going to do shit for my aching heart. But I still got dressed and went to the mall. It was the first place Duke and I had gone shopping together. Walking into Saks made me feel kind of sad about how things were going with us. I spotted Caroline, the saleswoman who had helped Duke and me the day he'd brought me here. She noticed me, but acted like she didn't recognize me. I walked up to her. Surely, she must've remembered me.

"Hello, Caroline," I said sweetly.

The old bitch crinkled her eyebrows at me. "Have we met?" she asked me.

"Yes, yes. I came in with Mr. Carrington, my boyfriend. You helped me pick out dresses and shoes," I reminded her.

She snorted a bit. "I'm sorry, I don't remember you. Mr. Carrington is accompanied by so many different women, I just can't keep it straight," the old bitty said sarcastically.

A hot feeling came over me. I didn't consider myself a violent person but I wanted to reach out and slap the shit out of this pompous, white bitch. I didn't fucking ask her who Duke came here to shop with. I was speechless. I couldn't move. It was as if I had been crazy glued to that spot in the store.

"Now would you like to open up your own personal shopper account? Because, I usually only help the women that are escorted by Mr. Carrington," the evil bitch said mockingly.

I could feel my face getting flush. The entire store began to spin around me. I gripped the counter for support and took a deep breath. I had to throw up. Composure was the word I was looking for . . . composure I didn't have at the moment.

I was finally able to move. I ran out of the store. My heels clacked against the mall tiles as I tried to get to my car before I lost my lunch all over the place. I was crying. I could feel a waterfall of tears streaming down my face. My body temperature soared. I felt faint. As soon as I made it to my car, I bent over and threw up. My face was a mess, a mixture of tears, snot and vomit. I was so weak and distraught. My worst fear had been confirmed. *Duke was cheating on me!* I didn't want to believe it, but now it all made sense. The day I had gone into Saks with him, Caroline's old white ass laughed at me. She knew I was one of many stupid ass women who fell for Duke Carrington's shit. Things were starting to slip fast.

I sat in my car for at least an hour before I could finally drive. The first place I went when I left the mall parking lot was to CVS. *I needed to find out why all of a sudden I was so sick.*

CHAPTER 15
DAMN, DAMN, DAMN

I raced back to the condo feeling and looking a mess. With my little pharmacy bag in hand, I went into the bathroom and fumbled out of my jeans. I sat on the toilet and ripped open the small box. My heart was hammering so fast I was almost out of breath. I pulled out the little white test stick and forced my urine out in a fast stream. I put the stick between my legs and when I thought I'd gotten enough piss on it, I set it on the side of the sink.

I was so nervous I started gnawing on my fake nail tips. "C'mon . . . c'mon," I urged, staring at the test. As if my utterances would make the results appear faster. The little window that turns pink when it was time to read the test results seemed to take forever. Finally, it was completely pink, which meant, it was time to read the results.

I inhaled deeply and picked up the little device. This was the new and improved test . . . the one that showed the words pregnant or not pregnant so there was no mistaking the results. And for sure, there was damn sure no mistaking what the capital letters read . . . PREGNANT.

I cupped my hand over my mouth. I didn't know whether to feel happy or sad. A baby! A fucking baby! Me, a mother! *Damn, damn, damn!*

All kinds of thoughts invaded my head. The final thought was that this could only be a good thing. Although Duke and I hadn't been together long, he had taken care of me and I knew he wouldn't turn his back on his own baby. He didn't have any kids or so I hoped. I figured a baby would make him very happy. Maybe this was what he needed to bring him home at nights and make him spend more time with me. Maybe if I gave him his only child, he would finally marry me. With that in mind I grew excited. *This baby would be the best thing for our relationship.* I told myself. I was excited.

I walked around the condo touching my stomach over and over again. I kept playing what I would say to Duke repeatedly in my mind. I definitely wasn't going to tell him over the phone. I would call him and tell him I needed to see him right away. I could just envision him snatching me up in a big bear hug and whirling me around. I was thinking he would shower my face with kisses and tell me to sit down, because he didn't want anything to happen to his precious baby.

The thoughts made me so antsy, I was going to call Duke and interrupt whatever he was doing. Yeah! That was what I decided to do. I could hardly contain my excitement as I dialed his cell phone number. I gripped my cell phone tighter and tighter each time Duke's phone rang on the other end without an answer. My stomach was in knots now. A feeling of dread and disappointment washed over me.

Then I heard his voicemail. "This muthafucka is ignoring my calls!" I screamed out loud. I ran my shaking hands through my hair. "He better answer this fucking time!" I dialed the number again. This time it went straight to voicemail. "Ok, maybe he is trying to call me back," I reasoned.

I hung up my phone and stared at it, waiting to see if Duke's call back would come through. I kept looking at the phone. With each minute that passed my blood pressure went higher and higher. I was fucking fuming mad now. "How does this bastard know if I'm calling for an emergency or not!" I screamed out.

I called Duke's number back again. It immediately went to voicemail. That meant he turned his phone off. After he saw my missed call, he had the nerve to turn his phone off. I threw my cell phone down on the floor and tossed the pregnancy test into the trash. My happy moment had once again faded to black. Without Duke, there was nothing to be fucking happy about.

After calling Duke's phone at least a dozen more times, I must have dozed off because I was startled by my cell phone's loud ringing. I jumped up and looked around. I was on the floor in front of the bed, where I must've cried myself to sleep. I went and picked up my phone. It had already stopped ringing. I knew it was Duke calling to tell me he was sorry for not answering my calls.

To my great disappointment, when I looked at my cell the screen read Diamond. I sucked my teeth. But I guess she would do. I pressed send to call her back. She answered on the first ring. Diamond was screaming into the phone almost breathless. I couldn't understand her at first, but then I heard his name.

Diamond had said Duke's name in the same sentence with the words . . . another bitch.

With my phone to my ear I raced towards the condo door.

CHAPTER 16
TOO MANY HOES

The tears were rolling down my face like waterfalls during my entire drive.

I drove with reckless abandon. I was speeding like a madwoman and I cut off more than one driver. When I finally pulled my car into the *Magic City* parking lot, I couldn't put it in park fast enough. I stormed through the club's doors and stopped. I moved my head left to right scanning for Duke's ass. My chest was heaving up and down and I was no longer upset, I was in *a blind fucking rage*. Finally, I saw Diamond rushing towards me. She had her hands out as if she was going to try to stop me.

"Wait, Lynise . . . wait!" Diamond cautioned me.

"No, fuck that Diamond! Where is he?" I screamed over the loud music.

"Let me just calm you down first. I don't want you to—" Diamond tried reasoning.

"Move!" I cut her off and pushed past her.

I knew right away where the fuck Duke was at. She didn't have to tell me. I stalked towards the champagne room. I could hardly breathe. I could hear Diamond running behind me. It was too late for all of that. I snatched the door open and I gasped at what I saw. I could see Duke sitting back on one of the leather sofas and the ass cheeks of the new stripper Diamond had told me about named Christa. She was standing on the couch straddling Duke's face. He had his hands on her ass pushing her towards his open mouth. This muthfucka was actually eating the pussy of a strange bitch! How fucking dare he! I was the one kissing him on the mouth. I had never been in that position with Duke. It was always straight up and down hardcore fucking.

I felt as if I was going to stop breathing. My vision became completely clouded with red. I clenched my fists together and I charged straight for them.

"Arrggghh! You muthafuckin' liar!" I screeched as I moved forward. I felt like I was possessed by the devil. The girl whipped her head around and screamed when she saw me coming straight for her, but it was too fucking late.

I snatched that bitch off the sofa by her long hair, which was a wig and it came right off. She was so shocked she didn't have time to break her fall or keep her wig on. She landed on the floor on her naked ass. I reached down and grabbed the little patch of real hair she had slicked back to put her wig on. With one hand I held onto Christa's real hair and with the other hand I started pounding her in the face. She tried to grab my hair but I was wailing on her ass so hard she couldn't see to grab my long ponytail.

"Lynise! Oh my God!" Diamond screamed out.

But I wasn't letting go of the bitch. I couldn't, no, I wouldn't let this bitch or any other bitch disrespect me.

Duke was busy trying to fix himself. The asshole had also begun taking his dick out of his pants when I caught him. His shit was literally open around his waist. I guess he was going to fuck the bitch too. The girl was screaming but I wasn't letting her go and I continued banging her in her face. Finally, I felt Duke grab me around my waist.

"Lynise, stop this shit! She ain't do shit to you!" he barked at me, finally able to pry me off his little nasty bitch. I had her hair all tangled around my hands and my knuckles ached from hitting her. I was out of breath and sweaty.

Perspiration donned my body from head to toe. Plus, I was still beyond pissed off. My reflexes made keen and I was still in *kick-somebody's-ass* mode.

"Oh, you gon' defend this bitch! Fuck you! You a nasty bastard! All that shit you talked about not being the strip club type of nigga! You're a fucking liar!" I screamed until my voice started cracking.

Duke let me go with a shove and I went stumbling. It was as if he was dismissing me. "Lynise, go home. I'll be there when I can," he said calmly, putting his hands up in a *talk to the hand* kind of motion. This bastard had the audacity to act cool and try to send me away like I was a child.

"Fuck you asshole! You're a dirty muthafucka! You think I don't know about the bitches in Saks and all that too, right? You piece of shit! You whack dick nigga!" I was trying to find any words that would make him feel even close to the amount of humiliation and hurt I felt.

"You hide behind your money and your fancy cars! But you ain't shit!" I continued my rant. "You come from shit and you ain't never gon' be shit! You gotta buy pussy! You think any of these bitches would give you the time of day if you was that same 'hood trash you were born as!" I was throwing his personal secrets he had confided in me during some of our dinner dates back in his face in public. I just wanted him to feel as embarrassed as I did.

Duke grabbed my face roughly. "Shut your fucking mouth!" he hissed. There was a crowd in the champagne room now. The security guards were trying to level with me to get me to leave. I wasn't having it.

"Your mama ain't want you! That's why you gotta buy women!" I continued, mumbling as he put pressure on my face. That was the last straw for Duke. He grabbed me by my hair and started dragging me from the club. Diamond was screaming for him to let me go. The security guards knew Duke and evidently knew him well, because they just let him drag me as if I was a rag doll. I should have realized then how big his ass was in the eyes of many, but a woman scorn is a woman who can't think straight in the heat of the moment.

"Get off of me! Owww!" I cried out in pain. Duke continued dragging me out the door. When we got outside he pushed me down to the ground right in the dirt of the parking lot. I was on my knees screaming and crying. All of my former co-workers from the club were outside watching the drama. Duke lifted his foot and kicked dirt on me. The dusty dry earth got on my face and in my hair, on my hands and knees. I started coughing and crying even harder.

"I picked you up from the gutter and the dirt, and bitch, I will send you right back if you ever disrespect me in public again. Now take your needy, funky ass home!" Duke spat, kicking me in the ass.

"Aggghhhhhh!" I screamed as I tried to pull myself off the ground. I didn't even have the strength to move. I actually felt as if I wanted to die rather than live with the utter embarrassment and shame I was feeling.

Diamond came over to me. "C'mon on, Lynise. I'm sorry about all of this. I can't believe this nigga," Diamond consoled as she helped me get to my feet. I grabbed onto her and just sobbed uncontrollably. Not only was I humiliated at how Duke had treated me in front of my co-workers, I was left with the reality that I was pregnant by him, a man who had no regard for women.

Diamond came back to the condo with me and helped me clean myself up. That's when I told her I was pregnant.

"Oh no, Lynise. After what happened tonight you need to be heading to the chop shop and getting that baby out of you," Diamond said flatly. I knew if it were under any other circumstances, she would have been very happy for me.

"How can you say that Diamond? He cheated yes, but he doesn't know about the baby yet. When I tell him, it might change things between us," I said, dabbing tears from my eyes.

"Do what you want, Lynise, but bringing another life into a fucked up situation is a big decision," Diamond began her lecture. "This nigga just cheated on you in a public place. Then he kicked dirt on you, literally and kicked you in the ass. Obviously, he is not the man you thought he was . . . a real man ain't gon' do no shit like that."

I couldn't even look at her because her words were driving a knife in my heart.

"Just remember our fucked up childhoods with no good ass fathers," Diamond reminded me.

She had a point.

But I was still holding onto hope that once Duke knew about the baby he would come around. I was really thinking that as soon as he knew he would make me his wifey.

Diamond made sure I was all right and then she got ready to leave. I gave her a long hard hug and thanked her for everything. When she left, my feelings went from sorrow to straight unadulterated anger. I kept playing the club scene over and over in my mind. I was stupid repeating the worst day of life in my mind. That thought coupled with me replaying the voice of the old bitch ass saleswoman at Saks mocking me made me feel even worse.

I stormed into the den, unlocked Duke's desk and took even more money out of his lock box. Usually, I would only take a few of the bills from the middle so he wouldn't really notice, but this time, I said fuck him and took two whole stacks of money. I was sure it had to be at least a couple of thousand dollars. I also picked up some of his business papers, household bills and some business contacts. I took all the stuff and stashed it away in a secure place amongst my things.

Just as I finished hiding everything, I was startled by the condo door slamming. I jumped and rushed over to the bed before Duke could come into the room. "Shit," I huffed under my breath thinking that was a very close call. I wasn't expecting Duke to come to the condo after everything that had happened. I was sure he would leave me in the condo alone for the night.

Duke came into the room and headed straight for the bathroom. At first, I tried to will myself to stay calm, but my emotions got the best of me. I couldn't keep it together any longer. I didn't know if it was my hormones from being pregnant or what, but I busted out crying in the bed. I got up and tried to go into the bathroom to talk to Duke but he had locked the door. I began banging on the door and screaming for Duke to open it.

"Duke, how could you do this to me!" I roared through my tears. "I gave up everything for you! You humiliated me! I can't believe you!" My throat was burning from screaming so much.

Finally, he opened the door. I looked at him out of my red, swollen eyes. His facial expression was like stone. "Lynise, if you ever embarrass me like that again in public, you will be out of my life. I will not tolerate that bullshit drama. I'm not up for it," he said all nice and calm.

I was stunned at what he said to me. It took a minute for his words to register in my mind. And his stone-faced expression was intimidating. But I stood my ground.

"How could you act like I did something to you!" I screamed through more tears. "You were fucking cheating on me in the place I used to work! In front of all my friends and former co-workers!"

"I thought you were ready to move on," he replied. "What's done is done. I don't want to hear all of this bullshit screaming and crying. I thought fucking with you was gonna be drama free. I thought you were a real woman and could handle a real man. I guess not. I gotta go."

His words really cut like a dagger through my fragile heart. I bent over and cried some more. It felt like he had actually stabbed me in the heart. "How could you!" I wailed. I had fallen to my knees again. My legs were too weak to stand.

"Grow up Lynise. Or get your own shit and get the fuck outta mine. Oh wait, you can't because you ain't got shit . . . everything you got I gave you. If you want to keep it that way then stay the fuck out of my way and just go with the flow."

With that, he exited the room and slammed the front door behind him.

I fell back on the bed and let the tears run. I still hadn't been able to tell him that I was carrying his child. One part of me wanted to pack up my shit and leave.

I didn't know if I could just accept Duke's blatant disrespect, but another part of me was convinced that when I broke the good news to him about our baby he would jump for joy and finally put a ring on it.

CHAPTER 17
IT AIN'T PERSONAL

I woke up the next morning to a ringing phone. I jumped up hoping it was Duke calling to apologize to me for his horrible attitude and behavior. But it wasn't him. It was Diamond again. This time she was checking in on me.

"What's up, Diamond? I'm fine," I mumbled, my voice still groggy with sleep.

She immediately went for the jugular, asking me that important question, whether or not I had told Duke about the baby? I told her the truth that I didn't tell him yet. Diamond went on and on about not telling him about the baby and to just get rid of it. For some reason she didn't see it like I did. Maybe hindsight is twenty/twenty, but at the time, I thought the baby was all I had left to save my relationship with Duke.

I quickly got off the phone with Diamond. I wasn't in the mood to hear what she was talking about that early in the damn morning.

I toyed with the idea of calling Duke and just telling him the news over the phone, but I really wanted to see him. I wanted to watch his reaction when he found out. I wanted to be the recipient of his hugs and kisses. I wanted to feel his excitement. Those visions of Duke's fantasy reaction quickly faded from my mind when I remembered that he hardly ever answered my calls and he had just cursed me out and treated me like shit. I sighed loudly and stared at my cell phone. From how things looked, I finally settled in my mind that I would be telling Duke the news via telephone.

It took me three starts and stops to finally place a single call to Duke.

When he answered his phone, my heart immediately started pumping wildly. When his voice filtered through the phone I could tell he was annoyed with my call.

"Duke, I don't want to fight. I want to talk to you . . . in person," I said in a low voice.

"Lynise, I can't come there right now. I'm taking care of business," Duke said dryly. He sounded like he hated my guts now. He wasn't even referring to me as Beautiful anymore. I was just plain ole Lynise to him now.

"Please, Duke. I'm begging to see you. I have to tell you something important," I implored. I had sat up in the bed. My head was spinning and I felt like throwing up. The morning sickness was coming on with a vengeance.

"Naw, I'm not up for no emotional bullshit today," Duke snapped. "You gon' have to tell me over the phone or don't tell me at all."

I closed my eyes and shook my head. I swear it was like this man went from an angel to the devil himself all in a matter of days. I just couldn't believe how he was speaking to me and treating me all of a sudden.

I swallowed hard and reluctantly proceeded to give him the news over the phone. "Duke, I'm pregnant," I said, almost whispering.

I heard him breathe hard like he was annoyed. He didn't say anything.

"Did you hear what I said? I'm pregnant with *our* baby!" I repeated in an urgent tone, my voice much louder now.

"Look, what you want me to say? I ain't got no kids for a reason, a'ight. So what you gon' do?"

His question felt like a slap in the face and his reaction felt like a kick in the gut. I was fighting hard to keep my composure. I didn't want to start yelling and screaming, but I sure felt like it.

"What do you mean what am I going to do?" I snapped back with attitude. "I thought you'd be happy. It's our baby. Duke, this baby was conceived out of love. I'm not some teenage girl that you need to ask what I'm gonna do." I was fucking offended and devastated. This was followed by the tears falling. I took a deep breath.

"I'm not gonna be happy about no baby. I'm a businessman and I'm busy," Duke said coldly. "I ain't got time to raise no kid. Look, if it's money you want, I got that. I really don't care what you do with that baby."

"That baby?" I screamed at him. "Duke, it is your fucking baby too! You are a real cold bastard! God don't like ugly—" Then I heard the phone go dead. Duke had hung up on me. I composed myself and decided I wouldn't shed any more tears over this shit. I was just going to handle my business and some of Duke's business too. He didn't know who he was fucking with.

I spent a week crying and not eating before I finally realized I was stronger than that. It seemed like after I told Duke about the baby he spent even less time coming to the condo. I hadn't seen him in over a week.

I pulled myself out of bed on a Saturday morning, showered and woke up with a new attitude. I decided I was going to be Duke Carrington's woman if it was the last thing that I did. I was determined. After I had a full breakfast for the first time in a week, I quickly made myself an abortion appointment. If Duke didn't want a baby, I wasn't going to force one on him. I had a new found fervor to give Duke everything he wanted. I wanted things to be exactly how it was when we first met.

My appointment was next Tuesday. Enough time for me to get my matted, nappy ass hair done. I needed both a manicure and pedicure. I wanted to look real good when Duke came to the condo. Since he hadn't been here in a while, I was expecting him any day.

I called Diamond and she met up with me. We did a day of Beautiful and shopping and I was feeling slightly happy again. That is, until my cell phone rang with a strange number. I picked it up all excited thinking Duke had gotten a new phone number and was calling me to apologize or tell me he thought about it and was really happy about the baby.

"Hello!" I sang into my phone.

"Is this Lynise?" the woman's voice filtered through the phone. My face immediately turned icy. There were no chicks with my number except Diamond and she was sitting across from me looking in my mouth.

"Who is this?" I snapped in a harsh whisper.

"I know you're fucking Duke and staying in the condo I used to live in. Well, I'm just letting you know, I'm living in the big house, and me and Duke are getting married in two months. I want you out of that condo because once I become Duke's wife I plan on selling it," the woman rambled like she was rushing to get the words out.

"Fuck you bitch! I'm with Duke and until he puts me out of the condo I ain't goin' no fucking where!" I belted out.

Diamond's eyes grew wide and she tried to grab the phone, so she could curse the bitch out too. But the woman had already hung up.

"Oh no Lynise. This nigga has gone far enough," Diamond barked. "He got bitches calling you now? It's time for you to either bounce or put the fucking screws to his muthafucking ass!"

"I just can't believe how he went from a dream to a nightmare. Why didn't he just leave me alone in the club and let me go on with my life if he knew he was going to be so fucked up," I lamented.

"I just heard rumors that he was getting married but you know how Virginia Beach is . . . so I didn't even pay that no fucking mind," Diamond confessed. "Geneva, the new hairdresser, is supposed to be doing all of the bridesmaids' hair . . . or so the rumor goes."

"Diamond, why the fuck you always wait until some shit jump off before you tell me these things!" I yelled at her.

"Because a real friend isn't going to report shit until I see it with my own eyes!" she replied. "Didn't I call you when I saw him up in the club?"

I nodded. She was right. "What am I going to do?" I asked, confused.

"Girl, I don't know what the hell you gonna do. What can you do to a man who has so many businesses, homes and so much money? It ain't much you can do . . . unless you plan on sending your baby daddy to jail for illegal adoption."

She reminded me of just one of the weapons I could use against Duke. When she said that it was like a light bulb had gone off in my head. I knew just what Duke needed . . . to be taught a lesson.

I stood up frantically. I must've startled Diamond because her eyes got wide. I threw some money down on the table for her to pay the bill.

"Diamond, I gotta go! I will talk to you in a few days," I said in a huff. With that, I raced to my car.

I had business to handle.

CHAPTER 18
MOMENT OF CLARITY

I sat behind Duke's desk inside the den of the condo as if I was really taking care of business.

I felt important and stately sitting behind the thick oak desk in the leather executive chair.

"Hi, is Mr. Barrett available?" I said to the woman on the other end of the phone.

"Ok, this is Mr. Carrington's secretary and I'm calling to cancel their meeting for tomorrow regarding the new real estate venture," I lied to Mr. Barrett's secretary. "Mr. Carrington asked me to give Mr. Barrett a special message, 'Fuck off crook!'"

I could tell the secretary on the other end of the line was taken aback. Duke would never be able to do business with real estate mogul Arnold Barrett again.

"Next up," I said evilly as I shuffled through Duke's business contacts and his calendar. "Ewe, this is a good one," I cackled as I dialed another number. "Good morning.

I am the spouse of Mr. Duke Carrington. I am calling to cancel all of our insurance policies with your company."

"Yes, homeowners, business and all cars," I lied to the customer service representative, in response to his question. "With a few exceptions. Uh, yes. Keep the insurance on the condominium at the Cosmopolitan building and the BMW X6."

"Oh, there is more than one BMW X6 listed," the customer service representative caught me by surprise. "Ok, well keep it on the candy apple red one," I said really annoyed. Then the bitch told me both were candy apple red. I was starting to feel like a fool. Duke had bought one of his other bitches the same fucking car.

"Ok, I will give you the VIN for the one to keep," I grumbled. I started fumbling with my pocketbook for the registration to my car. I read off the long vehicle identification number to the lady.

"Yes, that will be all. No, you cannot ask why we have cancelled our policies with your company!" I snapped and hung up the phone.

I put my head in my hands for a minute. Duke just didn't know who he had fucked with. "Next, cancelling his liquor license, all of his light and gas at his other homes, all of his upcoming meetings . . . and if he fucks with me, my next stop will be the police station with these fucking pictures."

I opened up the folder I had just found that contained photos of young pregnant girls, along with medical records and pictures of newborn babies. The folder also had dates of when the babies were sold, how much this bastard had sold the babies for and the rich muthafuckas who had bought them. When Duke had locked this folder up at the condo, I guess he was trying to hide it from his precious fiancée who claimed she lived at his mansion. Well, he underestimated me, the hood rat he picked up from the dirt, as he told me. I was about to bring this nigga to his knees. I planned on keeping the folder as my big gun to use at a later date. In the meantime, I continued my secret assault on all of his business ventures and personal life.

I picked up my cell phone and dialed another number. "Hi, yes, this is Mr. Carrington's secretary, I'd like to tell you that your lease at his building is being terminated," I lied yet to another person.

"No, we will not accept an extra thousand dollars a month rent, we want you out by the end of the week, thanks," I said in response to the counteroffer. I had to laugh when I hung up the phone. Everybody I had called so far was always shocked to hear the bad news. This shit was amusing. Duke's money was going to start drying up real fast. I had taken even more money out of his precious lockbox. My stash bag was damn near full. I was unleashing the heat on Duke's ass. I just needed to take care of a few more things before I officially got the fuck out of dodge.

I had my abortion at the clinic on Newtown Road in Virginia Beach, without telling Duke shit. I planned to continue walking around like I was pregnant so I could take that fucking bastard for every dime I could get out of him. When I got home from the clinic I felt a little weak, but other than that I wasn't feeling anything. I wasn't really bleeding that much. As soon as I walked in the condo, I knew Duke was there. The alarm didn't ask for a code and it didn't beep when I came through the door. I took a deep breath and prepared myself for what was to come.

Duke walked out of the bedroom and looked at me suspiciously. My heart started thumping.

"Where you been?" he asked me.

"Hi, Duke. I'm fine," I said sarcastically. "I haven't seen you in almost three weeks and the first thing you ask me is where have I been!" I snapped back.

"Answer the question," Duke retorted nastily.

"I was at the doctor. I needed to get something to take for my morning sickness . . . not that you care," I lied.

Duke seemed to soften a little bit when I said that. He dug into his pocket and pulled out a wad of cash.

"Here, this is for you and the . . . the—" Duke started but he couldn't say it. A four letter damn word and he couldn't spit it out. One simple word, four damn letters.

"The baby! The fucking baby, Duke . . . your baby!" I screamed, finishing his sentence for him.

"I didn't come here to fight," Duke replied. "I came to see how you were doing and to drop off some cash to you."

"Well, thank you for finally deciding I was worth checking on!" I barked. "Drop off some cash to me like I'm some cheap whore. I guess I am since you getting married in two months! Did you know that your new fiancé called me up to tell me you were getting married?"

Duke's black ass seemed to turn pale when I told him that.

"Why Duke? Why would you even bring me into this if you were with someone else?" I asked. I was trying so hard to fight off my tears.

"Because I want my cake and I want to eat it too," Duke said matter-of-factly. "I pay like I weigh so I'm able to have any woman I want . . . and if I decide to have a hundred that's what I will do. I take care of you and as long as I make money and give you some, you shouldn't have a problem with what I do." He was dead ass serious with that bullshit too.

"You ain't never heard the song, 'she ain't nothing but a gold digger . . . she ain't messing with no broke niggas?' That's all of ya'll women so as long as a nigga got money I'm gon' keep fucking with ya'll trifling ass gold diggers. Seems to me, ya'll got the best pussy anyway," Duke said, laughing evilly.

"You ain't never heard the saying it's cheaper to keep her?" I retorted. "Well, you better take heed to that one because in some cases . . . we ain't all gold diggers." I walked away from Duke and went into the bedroom and slammed the door.

When I was sure Duke had left, I ran into the closet and checked my stash. It was still there, untouched. I wiped sweat from my head, relieved that Duke hadn't found it. Now that I had gotten rid of the baby, it was time for me to start putting my Plan B into action. I knew it wasn't going to be long before Duke found out about what I had done to his businesses. I sat down in the closet and starting counting the money I had taken. I had amassed close to ten thousand dollars. Shit, that even surprised me. I hadn't even been stealing from Duke that long.

When I was finished counting and hiding the money, I called Diamond. Once again, she dropped a bomb on me. She told me she had heard Duke was having his engagement party at an exclusive country club in Virginia Beach, not too far from the damn condo I was living in. I didn't even get mad or upset like I usually did. I had long since left those emotions behind me. Now, it was all about getting even.

I called some dudes from the 'hood I grew up with. I told them there would be all kinds of luxury cars outside of the country club and I wanted every one of the cars to be destroyed, stolen or vandalized in some way that would cost the owners a fortune to fix. Once I started rattling off car types—Escalades, BMWs, Porsches—it didn't take long to convince my little wannabe gangsta friends to get to work. They knew just where to get the most money for those types of car parts. There were chop shops all over Virginia Beach.

With that being done, I set out to do more damage to Duke's life. My next deed was to fuck up his bank accounts, investments and really destroy him financially.

If I couldn't have the fucking money as his wife, nobody would.

CHAPTER 19
THE BREAK-UP

Three days had passed and I still hadn't heard anything from Duke.

He hadn't been back to the condo and at this point I didn't want to see him. The streets were buzzing about his impending marriage. Then I received a call from him.

"Hello," I answered.

"Bitch! You better be gone when I get back to town. I want you the fuck out of my condo and out of my fucking life," Duke barked into the phone. A cold sweat broke out all over my body.

"What are you talking about Duke?" I screamed, acting like I didn't know what was going on.

"You a lying ass bitch! You ain't pregnant bitch! I know you had a fucking abortion. I also know you been fucking with my money and my business! That shit ain't gon' be tolerated . . . now, if you wanna live, I suggest you be the fuck out of my place when I get there!"

I couldn't get a word in edge wise. I was on my feet pacing now. I was nervous as hell, but I knew this day was coming. That's why I had changed the fucking locks on the condo and put Plan B into action. I told Diamond I was leaving town. I didn't think it would be this soon. It was time for me to get my shit together and break out. Duke had threatened to come put me out before but he had never shown up, so I wasn't even scared.

I took my time walking through the condo putting shit together that I wanted to take with me. I had called around to a few apartment spots in Newport News and other parts of Virginia. I was leaving the Virginia Beach area for good. There was no way I could stick around after the humiliation Duke had put me through.

I had put the last of my things in my Louis Vuitton luggage that Duke had bought me when he sent me on an all-expense paid trip to the Caribbean when I was startled by a loud bang at the front door. I jumped. I crinkled my eyebrows and listened intently. That's when I heard the bang again. I put my hand over my mouth. I had been completely wrong. It was Duke! And he was trying to take the fucking door off the hinges to get to me.

"Bitch! You better open this fucking door!"

When I heard his voice, the banging and then the kicking on the door, my heart sank into the pit of my stomach. A hot flash came over my body at the sound of his deep, baritone voice. I could tell he was more than livid. I immediately started rushing through the luxury high-rise condominium where I had been living for the past six months. It was indeed his fucking condo and he was making sure I knew that. It was time to put my Plan B into motion. Quick, fast and in a hurry.

"Damn, damn, shit!" I cursed as I gathered shit up. I didn't know how I had let myself get caught slipping. I planned to be the fuck out of dodge before Duke could get wind of my deeds. I had definitely not planned my escape correctly.

"Lynise!" Duke's voice boomed again with additional angry urgency. He started banging even harder and jiggling the doorknob. I was scared as shit, but I wasn't shocked. I knew sooner or later he would come. After all the shit I had done to him, I would've come after my ass too.

"Lynise! Open this fucking door now!" Duke continued to bark from the other side of the door. He didn't sound like the man I had met and fell in love with. He damn sure didn't sound like he was about to shower me with cash and gifts like he used to. Not after all the shit I had done . . . or undone I should say.

"Open the fucking door!" he screamed again.

I was shaking all over now. From the sound of Duke's voice I could tell he wasn't fucking around. The last time he yanked my ass out of the club by my hair and he wasn't even half this mad. I could only imagine what he wanted to do to me now.

"Shit!" I whispered as I slung my bag of money over my shoulder and thought about my escape. I whirled around aimlessly but soon realized that my Plan B didn't include Duke being at the front door of his fifth floor condo. There was nowhere for me to go. It was only one way in and one way out and I damn sure wasn't jumping off the balcony. If it was the second floor, maybe I would've taken a chance but I wasn't trying to die.

"Fuck! Fuck! Fuck!" I cursed as I saw my time running out. Duke was a six foot tall hunk of solid muscle. I knew I had no wins.

"Bitch! I'm about to take this fucking door down!" Duke screamed. This time I could hear him hitting the door hard. I couldn't tell if he was kicking the door or putting his shoulder into it. Although it was his condo, I had changed the locks to keep his ass out.

I spun around repeatedly, trying to get my thoughts together before the hinges gave in to his brute power. Hiding the money I had stolen was paramount. My mind kept beating that thought in my head. I raced into the master bedroom and rushed into the walk-in closet. I began frantically snatching clothes off the hangers. I needed to use them to hide my bag of cash.

Wham!

"Oh my God!" I blurted out when I heard the front door slam open with a clang. I threw the bag onto the floor and covered it with piles of designer clothes. Things Duke and I had shopped for together when shit was good between us.

"Bitch, you thought I was playing with you?" Duke's powerful voice roared. "Didn't I tell you, you had to get the fuck out of my crib?"

He was up on me within seconds. I stood defenseless as he advanced on me so fast I didn't even have time to react. I threw my hands up, trying to shield myself from what I expected to come when he reached out for me. But I was too late. He grabbed me around my neck so hard and tight I could swear little pieces of my esophagus had crumbled.

"Duke, wait!" I said in a raspy voice as he squeezed my neck harder. I started scratching at his big hands trying to free myself so I could breathe.

"What bitch! I told you if you ever fucked with me you wouldn't like it!" he snarled. "You had all my shit cancelled! You fucked with my money! You had my house burglarized because you cancelled by fucking alarm system!

Huh, bitch? You tried to destroy me!" Tears immediately rushed down my face as I fought for air. "Ain't no use in crying now. You should've thought about that shit."

Duke finally released me with a shove. I went stumbling back and fell on my ass so hard it started throbbing. I tried to scramble up off the floor, but before I could get my bearings I felt his hands on me again. His strong hand was winding into my long hair.

"Ouch!" I wailed, bending my head to try to relieve some of the pressure he was putting on my head.

Duke yanked me up by my hair. Sharp, stabbing pains shot through my scalp.

"Owww!" I cried out as he wrung me around by my hair. I tried to put my small hands on top of his huge, animal hands, but it was no use. Hands I had once loved, I now despised and wished would just fall off.

"You thought it was all good right! You a fucking trifling ass bitch and I want you the fuck out of here before I kill you with my bare hands!" Duke gritted. Then he lifted his free hand and slapped me across my face with all his might.

"Pl-pl-pl-please!" I begged him for mercy. But Duke hit me again.

I was crying hysterically. Partly from the pain of his abuse, but more so from our past. I would have never thought our relationship would come to this. It had been a long road and all I wanted to do was teach him a lesson when I did the shit I did. I never thought I would have been facing this type of torment.

"I want all your shit out of here, you scandalous bitch! And don't take nothing that I fucking bought!" Duke roared, then he hit me again. This time I felt blood trickle from my nose. My ears were still ringing from the previous blow to my head. He hit me again. I was sure he had knocked one of my teeth loose.

"Yo Ak, get this bitch shit and throw it the fuck out," Duke called out to one of his boys. He never traveled anywhere alone, except when he used to spend the night. Other nights when he treated me as if I was a booty call, I was sure his boys were outside waiting for him. The one I knew as Chris rushed into the closet and started scooping up my clothes and shoes.

"Wait!" I screamed, but it was for nothing.

"Shut the fuck up!" Duke screamed in response, slapping me again.

I could actually feel my eyes starting to swell. I finally gave up. My spirit was broken, my body was sore. I watched as Chris and another one of Duke's boys slid back the glass balcony doors and started tossing all my shit over. I doubled over crying. More and more shit went over and I was sure it was raining down on the beautifully manicured law below.

"Yeah . . . that's enough. Don't throw none of that jewelry or those furs over. I got bitches I could give that shit to," Duke said maliciously. His words hurt. "A'ight bitch . . . your time is up."

I shrunk back thinking he was going to hit me again. But he didn't. He grabbed me by the arm roughly. "Oww!" I cried out. Duke was squeezing my arm so hard the pain was crazy.

"Let's go," he said, pulling me towards the door.

"Nooooo!" I screamed and then I dropped my body weight down towards the floor so he couldn't pull me.

"Oh bitch, you getting the fuck outta here," Duke roared. He bent down, hoisted me over his shoulder and started carrying me kicking and screaming towards the door.

"You can't do this to me! You will regret this Duke Carrington!" I hollered.

"Fuck you!" he spat in return, opening the condo door and tossing me out into the hallway like a piece of discarded trash. I can't even describe the feeling that came over me. It was a mixture of hurt, shame, and embarrassment all rolled into one.

Duke slammed the door in my face and I yelled for him to listen to me. My cries fell on deaf ears. My shoulders slumped down in defeat. Duke had left me in the hallway with no shoes, a short nightgown and nothing but my belongings on the lawn outside. I didn't even have the key to my BMW X6.

"Aggghhh!" I grunted in anger and frustration as raked my hands through my tangled hair.

It was by far not over yet.

I had more revenge left for his ass.

CHAPTER 20

NAKED

The Here and Now

My mind was flooded with thoughts of how I had gotten to this point.

My body was sore. My head hurt. My mind was fucked up. But somehow I had pulled it together to get out of there. I limped out of the Cosmopolitan condominium building half-dressed, with my face swollen and my hair a tangled mess.

I started gathering my things off the lawn. The first thing I tried to locate was my purse and my bag of money I had stolen. My purse was there, but that fucking money was history. My Plan B, my stash and all my hopes and dreams of becoming Mrs. Duke Carrington were gone. All I had left was a few designer dresses, handbags and shoes that were lying on the lawn.

As I picked up my things I could not stop sobbing. I picked up a pair of jeans and a t-shirt and slid them on. Of course I had attracted a crowd by now. Then as if he hadn't dissed me enough, one of Duke's little cronies came outside, got into my BMW and drove away. I felt like somebody had taken my heart out of my chest and stomped on it.

"Duke Carrington ain't heard the last from me," I mumbled to myself just as I looked down and noticed that the pictures and paperwork regarding the adoption ring was still in my purse, where I had put them earlier.

After I had all of my stuff together in one pile, I dug in my purse and got my cell phone. I called a cab and headed to the only place I could rightfully call home . . . or so I hoped. I prayed the entire cab ride that Diamond hadn't gotten one of the strippers from the club to be her roommate in my place. I felt so stupid running back to my old apartment with my tail between my legs . . . especially since I left there like I was on my high horse.

I dialed Diamond's number and prayed Brian wasn't at the apartment with her. She was a totally different person around him. My heart was racing as I waited for her to pick up. She finally did and I just lost it. I cried and cried and cried. It was so bad Diamond couldn't understand a word I was saying. She finally made out that I was on my way back to the apartment. She was out but told me she would meet me there. I didn't have my keys anymore, so I hoped Diamond would beat me there. I really didn't want to be ass out, especially in my condition.

The cab finally pulled into the apartment complex and I dug deep in my purse. I didn't even have enough fucking money to pay for the cab.

"Mister, I only have twenty dollars but if you give me your card I swear I will call you and pay you later or tomorrow," I cried, sounding as pitiful as I felt.

"No!" the cabdriver barked. "You pay now or I will call the police!"

"Oh my God! What did I do to deserve this!" I screamed. With my hands shaking I called Diamond again. I was praying she had some cash to loan me. Before I could place the call, Diamond knocked on the cab window. My shoulders slumped with relief. I was never so happy to see her ass.

"Diamond, I don't have enough to pay him and he's threatening to call the cops. Please, loan me some cash," It was a pitiful sight. I had gone from high price shopping sprees, high-class spas and exclusive restaurants to begging for cab fucking fare.

"Girl, you know I got you," Diamond announced, digging in her purse.

She paid the cabdriver and helped me with my things. As I climbed the old, dirty, worn down stairs to my old apartment, a feeling of depression and shame washed over me. I was right back where I started from, only this time I was worse off. Now I didn't even have a fucking job to make my own money and Duke had taken all of his money back. Even the money he had rightfully given me was left in the condo when he lifted me up and tossed me out on my ass.

When I got inside the apartment I was even more depressed. I was so used to Duke's condo with the expensive furniture and beautiful artwork, that the drab, raggedy furniture and old ass walls in the apartment made me feel sick. It looked worse than I had remembered, plus Diamond wasn't the clean type. When I lived there, I was the one who always kept shit clean. I couldn't be choosey though, so I just sat my stuff down and flopped down on the couch.

"So, what the fuck happened?" Diamond asked, sitting on the raggedy recliner across from me. I couldn't even speak without crying. I relayed the entire story for Diamond.

"Oh shit, yeah, I heard about the thing with the cars," Diamond announced. She had just begun her rambling, so I was going to let her finish was once again failing to inform me about some shit.

"Those stupid muthafuckas tried to sell the parts back to a chop shop that Duke owned," she continued. "So he caught one of the kids and they told that it was you who had told them to go there and fuck up those cars. Girl, I meant to call you and tell you that I heard that but I was caught up in some dumb shit with Brian."

I rolled my eyes at her. Truthfully, I wanted to kick her trifling ass but she was the one who took me in. However, she was a trifling bitch at times.

"Diamond, don't you think that shit should have been top priority on your list!" I finally opened my mouth in an uproar. "I could've fucking gotten away if I had known that Duke knew what was up! I was planning on leaving but he got there before I could get out. He got all the money I been stashing!"

Sometimes I thought she was a damn retard. I loved her but she was dense as hell. If she didn't already strip for a living, I would recommend her ass to be a fucking stripper.

"I'm sorry, girl, I been busy," Diamond apologized. "So, what you gonna do now?" I thought her tone was kind of condescending, like she was a little happy that I had to come back groveling.

"I'm gonna move back in here and go get my job back. I guess I'm gonna have to make a living somehow," I lamented.

"You don't think Duke is gonna bother you anymore, especially after all the shit you told me you did?" Diamond asked.

"I don't know but I can't afford to just up and leave. I have nothing," I said sorrowfully. "All those months . . . as a matter of fact . . . a goddamn year and I ain't got shit to show for it and now Duke is about to get married and publicly humiliate me even more."

"Well girl, you win some and you lose some. I guess you better try to get back to work 'cause ain't nothing going on but the rent up in this camp here," Diamond said sarcastically.

I rolled my eyes at her. That was what I had to look forward to. This bitch throwing my failed relationship back up in my face, especially because I had given her such a hard time about her no good ass man over the years.

You win some and you lose some. What kind of bullshit was that? And it was bullshit!

"Well, you can go back to your old room. Lucky thing I didn't let Shayla move in yet. Now I'ma have to tell that bitch she gotta find some place to live. But anything for you boo," Diamond said, walking over and hugging me.

"This shit ain't over Diamond. I'm telling you I can't just let go like this . . . not this easily," I told her. "I have to bring this nigga to his knees. The shit I did wasn't enough. I'm gon' have to find a way to completely ruin him."

"Just be careful. I wouldn't be able to handle coming to your funeral now," Diamond laughed.

But I knew her she was dead serious. What she didn't realize was a fool is born every day and the day I was born, I wasn't that fool. However, I couldn't say the same for Mr. Duke Carrington.

You win some, you lose some. Fuck that bitch, I planned on *winning*.

Chapter 21
This Can't Be Life

I lay around the apartment for a week feeling so depressed that I hardly wanted to get out of bed to eat and wash my ass.

Diamond was doing her usual in and out act. Sometimes I believed that bitch was really on some kind of drugs. Hell, who could stay up four straight days and then crash like that? She was acting like a real crack head. The reason I knew was because my own mother was one and that was her M.O., *modus operandi,* doing that same bullshit.

Plus, we knew countless dancers in the game who couldn't help themselves. Those who got hooked on something needed drugs or alcohol to take the edge off. Marijuana was a good drug to get hooked on but for most that didn't do a damn thing. If anything, it gave them the munchies and they gained weight. Alcohol cut the edge but that induced sleep.

Nope, the hard shit, *crack,* was the drug that sharpened the senses in the worst way. First, it kept you on your feet for hours and days on end. Then it helped you to crash and crash hard. Finally, it made you paranoid as a whore in an unguarded prison with men who haven't seen a woman in twenty years.

However, Diamond and I had made a pact to never do drugs. It was especially important since we were working in a strip club, the number one venue for getting hooked on something to cut the edge.

As much as I loved Diamond, I didn't have time to worry about her. I hoped like hell she had her shit together.

I finally pulled myself together. Enough that I decided I would go and try to get my old job back. I borrowed Diamond's car while she was asleep of course, and drove over to the *Magic City.* I took a deep breath when I parked the car. I had to get ready to throw myself at Neeko's mercy and beg for my old bartending job back. Hell, I'm sure throwing myself on the mercy of the court would have been easier than throwing myself at the mercy of Neeko. Unfortunately, bartending was the only thing I knew how to do to make some money. When I walked in the club, I got more than my fair share of stares and snickers. Still, I held my head high and ignored them.

I went to Neeko's office and knocked on the door. He yelled *come in* before he knew who it was at the door. When Neeko looked up from his desk and saw that it was me, his facial expression went cold. He squinted his eyes and twisted his mouth. Not a good sign.

"What's up, Neeko? How you been?" I said, plastering a fake smile on my face. It was phony but I knew I had to try to get on his good side. I had essentially left the club high and dry without a good bartender. Duke had me so convinced I wouldn't ever need to work that I didn't even give Neeko the courtesy to call and quit.

"What the fuck you want?" Neeko grumbled, puffing on his stink ass cigar. I fanned my hand in front of my face to swipe away the stink smoke.

"Um . . . I was wondering if I could just go back to work. I know what happened was kind of fucked up and all but you know I'm good at what I do . . . I really, really need this Neeko," I said, begging without shame.

"Naw, I don't need nobody else. I got a new bartender and she's fine as shit and she don't gimme no lip," Neeko said dismissively.

"C'mon Neeko, I'm willing to share shifts. I'm willing to stay all the way until the last customer leaves. Anything, I just need a job," I begged some more. I was on the brink of tears and I was fighting hard not to cry.

"Naw, Lynise. I can't fuck with you right now," Neeko said with finality.

I stood there in shock for a minute. I guess I always thought I could just keep getting my way in life. I never thought I'd be on the desperate side of shit.

"You can be one of my strippers if you want. I always wanted to see that apple ass without clothes," Neeko said, blowing more cigar smoke in my direction.

I started coughing and gagging. "Fuck you Neeko! I ain't never taking off my clothes for a bastard like you!" I spat. As I turned to leave, Neeko called after me.

"Lynise! You might as well strip 'cause ain't much else you can do in these parts. Somebody done seen to that."

I flipped him the bird and stomped out of his office. I had no idea what the fuck he was talking about.

I peeled out of the parking lot in Diamond's car. "Fuck Neeko! There's more than one club in the Tidewater area!

I'm gonna be alright! I'm a damned good bartender." I drove to the next strip club.

When I got inside, the owner also dismissed me. He said some shit like he couldn't work with me even if he wanted to. I didn't know what the fuck he meant by that bullshit. I told him to kiss my ass and I headed to the next club. Same shit. The owner would hear nothing of hiring me. This shit was starting to really make me suspicious. When I got to the last club on my list I just knew I would get a job. It was owned by a guy named Drew and he and I had gone out way back in the day. I was really embarrassed when I walked into his club and saw his fine ass sitting inside with his iced out chain and pinky ring. I immediately felt small. I fought the feeling because I needed a job badly.

"What's up, Drew?" I said, flashing a smile. In my desperation, I tried using my strategy. While I was still in the car, I opened the top buttons on my shirt all the way down to my cleavage. I really was in desperation mode. *It is what was is.* If I had to show some breasts to get a job, then that's what I had to do.

"Ayyy, Lynise. Long time, no see, girl," Drew said. His enthusiastic reaction was a good sign. I was excited already.

"Well, you know I must be here for a reason, so let me just get right to it. Drew, I need a job like nobody's business right now," I said trying to make myself as seductive as possible. I knew Drew and he was always a little on the perverted side. I probably would've even rubbed up on him for a job at this point. Anything except suck his dick.

"Yeah, baby girl. I heard around town you was kind of down on your luck and shit," Drew said. When he said that a sharp pain immediately shot through my stomach. That meant all of my business was already getting around the Tidewater area. I was probably the fucking laughing stock.

"You know shit happens," I replied, trying to play the shit off. "But I'm also sure you've heard I'm the best female bartender around and I bring in the crowds. That's how good and strong my drinks are."

"I heard that but I can't help you baby girl," Drew said. He looked kind of hesitant though.

"Ugh!" I grunted, throwing my hands up. "Why is everybody dismissing me? So what, I had a falling out with my boyfriend, what does that has to do with me mixing fucking drinks!" I barked in frustration.

"Baby girl, I thought you knew the deal. Listen, I'ma tell you this for ya own good," Drew said, leaning in closer and whispering. I looked at him strangely, confused. "That nigga Duke Carrington holds a lot of weight in these here streets. He went around everywhere to all the bars across the city telling niggas not to fuck with you. Said you was a thief and couldn't be trusted. That nigga even threatened that if any of us put you on to a job, he was gon' have our liquor licenses revoked.

"You know he got peoples on the fucking board down there at the ABC. That's how the nigga found out you tried to get his liquor license fucked up. Word is, if so many people didn't know about you fucking up his business shit, he was gon' body you."

This shit made my ears start to ring. I wanted to just scream. Duke was the fucking reason I couldn't get a job. How dare this bastard. He was trying to play me at my own game. I tried to undo his life so now he was fucking up mine. If I had any kind of fucking sense, I should have been upset that Duke would have me killed if everyone didn't know how I tried to fuck him up.

"Ya'll don't know the half of it. But thanks for the heads up. I understand all ya'll little scary ass so-called men let Duke run ya'll . . . it's all good," I snapped at Drew.

"Hey, don't shoot the messenger. I can't fuck with you," Drew said flatly. "It took me a arm and leg to get my liquor license. I ain't about to risk that to hire no troublemaking bartender."

"Yeah, a'ight. You mark my fucking words. You, the rest of these sucka ass club owners and Duke Carrington ain't heard the last of Lynise! That nigga should've learned it was cheaper to keep my ass!" I screamed at Drew.

"You can go now with all that rah rah bullshit, Lynise. At least I told you the truth," Drew said, sounding frustrated with me. I couldn't blame him. I was taking out my anger for Duke on him.

I turned around and hurried my ass out of Drew's club. I couldn't wait to get outside. As soon as I stepped foot out of Drew's club, I picked up my cell, blocked my phone number and called Duke's ass. Surprisingly, he picked up. I couldn't control myself I was so angry.

"Duke! You sorry muthafucking excuse for a man!" I screamed into the phone. "Why the fuck are you going around to the clubs blackballing me?" I screamed into the receiver. I wouldn't even give him a minute to speak. I kept on with my tirade. "You ain't got shit else to do? You worrying about me? You so fucking weak that you threatened every club owner in the area not to hire me? Wow, it took a real man to do that! So how am I going to make money to take care of myself when you was the muthafucking reason I quit my job in the first place?"

I screamed so much and so loud my throat hurt. I was emotional and hurt and pissed off I ever got involved with this asshole.

The asshole finally opened his mouth and started talking. He was screaming as well, which meant maybe I got to him. "Listen, you two bit classless whore! I don't give a fuck how you support yourself. Bitch, you thought you was gonna use the money you stole from me, but you had another thing coming! Chris found that shit when he was throwing your shit out of the condo! You dumb bitch!"

I was trying to scream back at him but his deep voice was overpowering mine. "I'm telling you, Lynise, if you ever call me, come near any of my businesses or homes again, your crack head mama and your crack head, dick sucking, pussy selling, best friend is gon' find ya muthafucking head in one place and they gon' have to go on a fucking scavenger hunt to find the rest of your body parts. I done told you more than once, I ain't nothing to be fucked with," Duke said menacingly.

Then the phone went dead.

That bastard had hung up on me.

I started banging my fists on the car's steering wheel. I banged until my hands throbbed. I was so angry that if I had a gun I would've found Duke and shot him right in his head.

He had gotten this one, but I was going to find a way to get his ass back.

Chapter 22

Trouble

I was depressed and I knew it.

All I wanted to do was eat and sleep and in between I would have bouts where I just cried my eyes out for hours. I thought about Duke a lot. Sometimes I would drift into the good times we had. I would find myself smiling as I often went into the deep recesses of my mind to replay how Duke spared no expense when it came to spending time with me and making me happy. I sometimes still didn't believe shit had gone so wrong so fast. The shit Duke had done to me was just straight foul. I would never forget it either. He had made me turn on him, it was my defense mechanism.

My life had definitely gone from charmed to hell, *from sugar to shit.* I laid around the apartment for days and weeks, most of the time listening to Diamond and Brian either fucking or fighting. I went from my bedroom to the living room and back again. Diamond was starting to act a little funny because she was footing all of the bills. Although she said she understood my situation after what Duke had done to me, she still acted funny. Sometimes she would come in all drunk and shit and she wouldn't even speak to me. Sometimes I even heard her whispering on the phone about me not helping her.

I was lying on the couch feeling sorry for myself watching TV, which had become my usual routine. I was flipping channels and there were commercials on all of the local channels. I was so frustrated with that bullshit. It was crazy that we paid for cable every month and there wasn't ever shit on TV that I wanted to watch. I settled on Channel 4. Just in time to catch the news coming on. I decided to find out what was going on in the world since I had become a recluse. I was staring at the TV in a daze when I saw the headline flash the words *Breaking News*.

I didn't budge and it didn't make me sit up or alarm me at all because in the Tidewater area there was always breaking news. I watched as a female reporter flashed on the screen and started speaking.

I'm Carolyn Thomas and we have breaking news today. The police report that the body of a sixteen-year-old female teenager was found today in the woods near Highway 3. Investigators report that the girl's body had been severely mutilated and confirmed that it is evident the girl was pregnant prior to her death. Police say it looks like the girl suffered a botched cesarean section prior to her death. Police are not releasing any information about the fetus or whether or not a fetus was recovered with the girl's body. Sources also report the girl may have been homeless or a runaway. They are trying to identify the girl and determine if anyone had reported her

missing. Police are asking that if anyone has any in-
formation about this girl or any information that
could lead to her killer or the whereabouts of her
baby, please call 1-800-CRIMESTOPPERS."

I was sitting on the edge of the sofa when I heard the story. But when I saw the police sketch of the missing girl, for
some reason her face was familiar to me that my heart
started racing like I knew the girl personally. I swallowed
hard and jumped up off the sofa. It had struck me like
lightning. I just knew I had seen her before. I raced into my
bedroom to find my pocketbook. Something told me the
dead girl was in some way connected to that fucking shelter
where Dr. Gavin and Duke were running that baby scam.

"The fucking pictures I took from the condo," I whispered as I frantically turned my pocketbook upside down
and let everything fall on my bed. I started sifting through
the stuff on the bed as if I was crack fiend trying to find the
smallest amount of crack to keep the high going.

"Finally," I whispered. I grabbed the papers and pictures
I had taken out of Duke's desk at the condo. With my hands
shaking, I shuffled through them one by one. My heart was
throbbing rapidly. I looked at the first picture. It wasn't the
girl that was shown on the news. For some reason, I felt kind
of relieved. I flipped to the next picture. No luck. The
second picture wasn't the girl either. I let out a long sigh, but
my heart was still beating as if I had run around a track.

Ok, I was starting to think I was just crazy and wrong. I
kept flipping through the pictures though. When I got to the
third picture, my eyes popped open wide and I dropped the
entire stack of pictures as if I had been bitten by a snake. A
cold chill shot down my spine and an eerie feeling overcame

my entire body. My stomach knotted up. I put my hand over my mouth to keep myself from screaming.

I knew I had seen the girl shown on the news before and I was right. I had to be sure. I bent down and slowly picked the picture back up. I could hardly look at it good my hands were trembling so badly. I stared at the picture a good long while. There was no mistaking it. I was positive the sketch of the girl on the news was identical to the picture I had in my hand. I turned it over and read the back.

"Bastard," I gritted. Dr. Gavin had listed the girl's height, weight, eye color, hair color, nationality, expected due date and the sex of the baby she was carrying.

"These muthafuckas killed this poor girl and stole her fucking baby," I said to myself.

Duke and Dr. Gavin had probably sold the girl's baby before the baby was even ready to be born.

I was spooked to say the least. I kept looking at the girl's picture. She was a pretty little girl and she looked like she was of mixed heritage. I could only imagine how much money Duke must've gotten for what must've been a very pretty baby from the girl. The news reporter said it looked like the girl had suffered from a botched C-section. I couldn't even imagine the pain she must have suffered while Dr. Gavin cut on her and took the baby. I prayed he at least knocked her out before he did the procedure.

I couldn't concentrate or anything. "Damn, I don't know what to do." That was slowly becoming my thing, talking aloud to myself. How would I be able to live with myself knowing that I may have information about that poor girl and not turn it in? On the second hand, I had stolen the paperwork from Duke, which meant I would have to turn him in and I might implicate myself since I had spent his illicit money. So much shit was running through my head.

I paced around the apartment trying to wait for Diamond to get home. She would be my voice of reason . . . she always was. She would tell me the truth about whether going to the police with the information was a good idea or not. I knew if I went to the police they would have a lot of questions about how I got the pictures. Then they might try to implicate me for knowing about the illegal adoption shit and not reporting it. But then again, I hadn't done anything wrong.

These thoughts went back and forth in my mind like a ping pong match. I tried to weigh the pros and cons of turning Duke in, but I was way too nervous to reason. "He would be totally done if I did that."

Suddenly a light bulb went off in my damn head. This missing girl was going to be exactly what the fuck I needed to get back at Duke for how he treated me. If I could help the police tie the girl to Duke, he really would be done. His little life with his new wife and all of his money would be over. His damn face would be splashed all over the news. He would suffer the humiliation I suffered when he constantly dissed me in public. All of a sudden I felt a mixture of fear and excitement.

I had to call Diamond. I didn't care what she was doing, I wanted to tell her about this. I needed her to ride with me on this one. If I was going to go to the boys in blue on Duke, I needed a witness just in case something went wrong. Shit, somebody had to live to tell the story. For all I knew Duke might've had the entire police department working with him. I mean let's face it, he had enough money to buy the city, why not pay off a few cops.

I picked up my cell and dialed Diamond's number. It was ringing. "C'mon girl, pick up the damn phone . . . pick up dammit. I need you right now," I mumbled as I paced the floor of my bedroom with my nerves standing on end.

Diamond finally picked up her phone. I was happy for a few seconds. I crinkled my face because my ears were immediately assailed by all of the loud rap music in the background.

"Diamond! Go some place quiet! I need to speak to you about something very important!" I screamed into the phone. I don't even know why she would try to answer her phone inside the club with the music blaring. Diamond was laughing hysterically like something I was saying was funny. She kept laughing but at least the background noise finally got quieter. I assumed she went outside or downstairs in the club's dressing room.

"Wassup!" Diamond yelled into the phone. I had to pull the phone from my ear she had screamed so loud. I guess she still couldn't hear me as clearly as I could hear her.

"Diamond, I need to talk to you about something real important," I huffed. This bitch started laughing again. "Diamond! I'm not joking! What are you laughing at?" I yelled at her.

"Ok . . . ok. I'm serious now," Diamond slurred. I was too anxious to tell her what I knew to even pay attention to her slurring words and constant laughing.

"Girl, listen . . . have you heard about a sixteen-year-old girl that went missing?" It probably was a stupid question because Diamond never watched the news, but I figured maybe she heard something on the streets about it.

She told me she hadn't heard anything. I told her what I had just seen on the news. "Diamond, I swear I think that girl was one of those girls that Duke and that creepy fucking doctor had down at the shelter. Remember what we talked about . . . you know the baby snatching ring," I explained to Diamond. She was quiet for a minute.

"Diamond, I know Duke had something to do with this girl I just seen on the news," I said, but I didn't tell her I had the pictures and paperwork to corroborate my suspicions. I would never tell Diamond that information over the phone for fear she might repeat it in the wrong place and be overheard.

When I was finished telling her everything I suspected, this bitch busts out laughing as if I had just told her a joke. I had to pull the phone away from my ear and look at it because I could not believe my ears.

"Diamond! Are you listening to me?" I screamed again. "What the fuck is wrong with you? What is so funny?" I couldn't believe she kept laughing. That's when I realized my suspicions must've been right. Diamond was doing more than just having a few drinks, she must've been getting high off something. This reaction just wasn't like her.

Then to top it off Diamond told me I was being paranoid and that she always felt I was a little crazy. I felt betrayed. The only person I had left was even blowing me off. Diamond dismissed me and told me she had to get back to work. She made me feel like a silly nut case. That was a first coming from Diamond because she never blew me off to go show her ass.

When she hung up the phone, I was left all alone with my dilemma. I went back into the living room and flipped through the channels to see if there was something more on the mutilated girl. I stopped on Channel 7 news. The entertainment and gossip session was on and I was hoping maybe some real news would come on after this piece. But damn, what was on the screen shocked me. I was stunned. Two shockers in one night threatened to send me to the hospital with a heart attack.

Right before my very eyes was the media coverage of *Tidewater business mogul Duke Carrington's wedding to the daughter of a pastor.*

I bit my bottom lip when I saw Duke, all dressed in a tuxedo, kissing and smiling with his new wife. I felt nauseous watching them. I squeezed the TV remote until my hands hurt.

That was all I needed. "Fuck you Diamond. I'm not paranoid. And you, newly married mogul Mr. Carrington, you fucking low down dirty dog, your life as you know it will soon be over," I grumbled at the TV as the last few happy images of Duke and his new wife flashed across the screen.

I was fuming mad now. That was supposed to be my wedding with the news cameras showing footage of me and Duke canoodling and smiling.

I rushed and got dressed, picked up the pictures and the other paperwork I had taken from Duke's safe and I headed out.

I was on my way to the Virginia Beach police department. This time, I had enough information to ruin Duke for good.

Walking out the door I lied to myself believing this was closure for the young girl who had died a violent and useless death, and the lost of her child.

Deep down, I knew this was about me—*all about me!*

CHAPTER 23
THERE'S BEEN A MURDER

I was sick to my stomach the entire ride to the police station.

Diamond's little hoopty was smoking under the hood too. "Shit. No wonder she left this fucking car home." That would be all I needed to break down on the damn ride to the police station. Thank God, the car made it.

I pulled into the stationhouse parking lot and started having second thoughts about going through with it. I didn't know what I'd say when I got inside. I didn't know how I would sound saying, "Hey, I got information on a dead girl."

I started rehearsing stuff to say. "Excuse me, I saw a girl on the news and I have pictures of her and I know she has been a part of an illegal adoption scam and it was my ex-boyfriend," I rambled out loud nervously. That little practice didn't help.

"Shit, Lynise, that sounds dumb as hell," I scolded myself. I slammed my fists against the steering wheel in frustration. "Ok, get your shit together. Just go in there and tell them the truth." I was finally ready to do it. Duke was going to be sorry. I exited the car and went into the police station. My eyes grew wide once I was inside.

"Damn, I would come on the most crowded damn night," I mumbled as I looked around. There were people sitting, standing, yelling and crying. There was one lady sitting on the steps, in the damn way, with a crying ass baby. I heard her tell her friend she was waiting to post bail for her man.

I saw another chick sitting in one of the hard chairs filling out a complaint form. She was screaming on her cell phone telling somebody she was waiting to press charges against her man. Evidently he had beaten her ass and slammed her head on the concrete outside of her project apartment. When she finally looked up from her paperwork I could see what she was talking about. She had a fucking purple, green and blue shiner under her right eye. I shook my head in disbelief.

The police station was like a damn zoo.

I walked up to the little scratched up window to ask for help. "Excuse me, officer," I began. The fat female cop behind the plexiglass put her hand up to me like *talk to the hand*. I stopped what I was saying abruptly and looked at her strangely. She kept her hand up and her head down. I was getting heated.

Finally, she looked up with her triple chins. "What can I do for you?" the fat officer said dryly.

"I need to speak with someone regarding a missing person—" But once again the fat bitch cut me off.

"Has the person been missing for more than twenty-four hours," she asked in a rushed, nasty tone.

"What? No. I . . . I . . . I don't want to report somebody missing. I have information on a missing murdered girl I saw on the news tonight," I told her. She looked even more disgusted now. Probably because they had received too many false leads tonight or the fat cow finally thought she needed to do some work.

"Wait right here," the fat officer grunted. She picked her huge body up out of the small chair. I felt sorry for the damn chair. She called out to her sergeant, repeated what I said and then came waddling back to the window.

"You saw this on the news?" she asked. "Was it a crime stoppers story?"

"Yes, about a girl found dead with a botched c-section and a missing baby," I repeated. The officer let out a long sigh like I was bothering her.

"Just go have a seat and let me see if I can get a detective to come see you. I ain't promising you nothing," she said, dismissing me. I rolled my eyes and went back to the crowded waiting area to find a seat. There were no seats so I just stood against a wall.

I watched the people coming and going in and out of the station. There was some ghetto shit going on in the station-house. I had to move out of the way as two girls started fighting right there in the lobby. How bold was that? Assaulting each other in a police station. From what I could gather, they were both there to bail out the same dude. That nigga had apparently called both of his babymamas and both were there with kids around the same age. I watched as they both got their asses arrested, now neither one of them could bail out the man and both of them would have to later fight child protective services to get their kids back. I just shook my damn head. I couldn't wait to get the fuck out of that place.

It seemed as if the cops were calling everybody but me. I had finally got a seat but I was still waiting. I looked over at the fat cop and she rolled her eyes. It had been at least forty minutes and I still hadn't been seen. Now I could see why people didn't come down to make police reports. These cops were the worst.

The longer I sat there the more time I had to think. I started remembering things I had heard Duke say on the phone and I suddenly remembered him saying something he had a few cops on his payroll. The longer I sat there the more I had second thoughts about what I had come to the police station to do.

Then a real sinister thought popped into my head. *What if I told Duke that I had the pictures? That I knew about his scam with Dr. Gavin? And lastly, that he would have to give me some serious money to keep my mouth shut.*

Yeah! Blackmail that muthafucka!

Hell, just like that my plans changed. That's what I was going to do. Blackmail the fuck out of his nasty ass.

I jumped up from the seat I was in. I looked over at the fat bitch of a cop and I flipped that bitch the bird.

I hurried out of the police station with a mission on my mind. I was broke, busted and disgusted, but not for fucking long.

Duke Carrington would be giving me stacks for the shit I had on his ass.

CHAPTER 24
THE ALMIGHTY DOLLAR

I was feeling hyped up and bold when I rushed back to the apartment.

Blackmail and getting lots of money was on my mind. But by the time I got back home, my thoughts were dashed when I walked into the house to hear Diamond and Brian sounding as if they were having a wild damn party in Diamond's room.

I didn't know what the fuck was up with her lately, but her shit was getting out of hand. It was wild partying, disappearing acts or big horrible fights with Brian. This was the time I needed her most. I was desperate for a way to make money and at the same time I wanted to ruin Duke and his entire life. I was frustrated I couldn't get to Diamond when I needed her.

With the amount of noise coming from Diamond's room, I knew I wasn't going to get to tell her my plan. I went into my room and pulled out the pictures of the murdered girl, the other pictures, and the lists and paperwork I had kept. I

159 | CHEAPER *to* KEEP HER

reviewed everything and the more I read, the more confident I was that it was going to get me some big bucks from Mr. Carrington's ass.

I didn't want to think hard about the path I was about to take. I knew if I did, I probably would have changed my mind. Duke and the doctor had mutilated a young girl, and she had something they needed—a baby. I didn't want to think about what the fuck they would do to me if I gave them the opportunity. No, money was on my mind. Hopefully, stacks and stacks of money.

I lifted one end of my mattress and stashed the papers under it. I went into the kitchen and took four Tylenol PM. I knew without it I wasn't going to get any sleep. I could still hear Diamond laughing all loud and shit. I couldn't believe she was still with Brian after he beat her ass. I shook my head, took some cotton and stuffed my ears, and went to bed. I would have to see Diamond when that bastard of a man of hers was gone.

I tossed and turned all night. I kept dreaming that Duke was after me because of my plot to blackmail him. I could actually see his face curled into a snarl as he was coming after me. That dream had me jumping. I had broken out in a cold sweat. I was obsessing about everything, which wasn't good for my mental state.

When I saw the sun streaming through my blinds, I decided I might as well get up and start my day. I kept trying to get up, but my mind was in a repetitive loop. My plans were dominating my thoughts. When I thought I had moved my mind in another direction, thoughts of my plans would return. I just couldn't move on. I needed to talk to Diamond badly. I needed to share my plan and get her thoughts. Hopefully she would have words of reason.

I continued to lie in bed for a while when I finally confirmed that Diamond was up and about. I heard her turn on the shower. I figured Brian's ass was probably gone and now we had a chance to talk without any interruption. He usually left real early whenever he stayed over. I had once told Diamond I believed that nigga was married because of the way he would creep out at three or four in the morning.

After a few minutes, I decided to get up and go sit on the toilet while Diamond was in the shower so I could talk to her. I figured it was probably the only time I was going to have with her ass, since she was hanging out without me a lot lately. I padded through the apartment and opened the bathroom door.

"Diam—" I called out as I walk into the bathroom. Immediately, I almost choked on my words. My eyes grew wide and I was kind of stuck on stupid when I realized I had walked in on Diamond and Brian fucking. She was moaning loudly and had her hands on the shower wall, while Brian had her bent over slamming into her ass like a plow driver, fucking the shit out of her. I felt a pang of jealously come over me. I hadn't had a man's touch in a long while and all of a sudden I forgot why I had even come into the bathroom. I was suddenly missing Duke very much.

Diamond and Brian both turned and looked at me as if I was crazy. I don't know why my feet wouldn't move. I was stuck in imaginary mud, watching them instead of turning around and getting my ass out of there.

"Bitch, do you mind?" Diamond shouted indignantly. She had every right to yell at me. Brian didn't even have any shame. He just kept on fucking Diamond from the back with me standing there, unable to move.

"Damn, I thought you were in here alone. I'm sorry," I apologized as I was finally able to move and come to my senses. I hurriedly backed out of the door and slammed it shut.

"This bitch can't fucking knock! Non-paying rent ass bitch!" I heard Brian comment as I left the bathroom. His words seared right through me and fucking pissed me off. The audacity of that no good ass nigga, who didn't do shit for Diamond.

When I thought about what he had said and his past behavior, I banged my fists on the door. "Fuck you Brian! Ya'll should've locked the fucking door anyway! Shit, I live here too and I gotta take a fucking piss! Diamond got a bedroom to fuck in!"

I fucking hated that muthafucka. Hell, I think at that moment I fucking hated men.

I went back to my room and flopped down on my bed. I was even more motivated to get my plan underway now. Blackmailing Duke was the order of the day, because I needed to get some money. I definitely needed to get out on my own. It seemed as if Diamond and I were growing apart and going our separate ways in life.

I started running through my mind how much money I was going to demand from Duke's ass. I needed enough to give myself a brand new start in life. Fuck Virginia Beach! I needed to get the fuck out of this area. Hell, I probably needed to leave the state. In the back of my mind, the thought of the young girl being mutilated still lingered with me.

I started plotting how I was going to get this money from a powerful ass dude like Duke and remain safe at the same time. It was a lot to think about. Trust me, my mind was racing a mile a minute. My head ached from thinking so damn much.

After lying there thinking for several minutes, I heard Diamond and her piece of shit man come out the bathroom. I could actually hear Brian's hard ass footsteps going towards Diamond's room. I just rolled my damn eyes and stared up at the ceiling. I was still thinking about my dilemma when I heard a small tap on my bedroom door. I leaned up on one elbow and looked at the door. "Who?" I called out, knowing damn well who it was.

Diamond peeped her head inside. I gave her a mean look and flopped back down on my bed. She smiled at me and came and sat on my bed. I couldn't stay mad at Diamond's ass for long. She always knew how to make up with me whenever we had a little dust up.

"Girl, don't be mad. You know how Brian is and we were just caught off guard," Diamond said apologetically. "He ain't mean nothing by what he said . . . you know about the bills and stuff. I got on his ass about that."

I twisted my lips. "Yeah, but you know we always talk while one or the other is in the shower, so I was just trying to tell you about this shit that's going on with Duke. I wasn't trying to bust in on ya'll on purpose like he was making it seem."

"I know . . . I know you wasn't. Now what's this shit with Duke?" Diamond asked. But before I could answer her she started talking again. "Oh yeah, wait a minute, now I remember you called me at the club last night after my first set. I kind of remember you talking some crazy shit about some dead girl and some baby . . . Duke and the doctor. I believe you said a girl was on the news and her body was found or some shit. I mean, you sounded like a mad woman. And I wanted to ask you what the hell was you smoking on, girl. I couldn't believe that shit you was saying," Diamond said, laughing afterwards.

"You think this shit is all a joke?" I asked seriously. "I was dead ass serious! I'm telling you Diamond, I'm on to something here. I saw a girl on the news who was missing and found dead. She had been given a c-section and now her baby is missing. And I mean, stolen Diamond!"

I looked her in the eyes. Then I said, "Get up for a minute." When Diamond stood up, I lifted the edge of my mattress and retrieved the pictures and the paperwork that would confirm my suspicions and explain to her what I was trying to say. "Look at this shit Diamond," I passed her the stack of photos.

Diamond grabbed them and shuffled through the stack. Her face was deadpan. No emotion or reaction. "And?" she asked, twisting her lips. She had a so what, what the fuck look on her face.

"And . . . this girl right here, was on the fucking news," I said, plucking the picture of the dead girl, emphasizing my point. "She was found dead . . . murdered from a botched C-section! How many times I gotta explain this shit to you! These pictures came from Duke's condo . . . his desk! Now you tell me I shouldn't be suspicious that he had her killed or even worse, killed her himself so he could snatch her fucking baby!"

"What?" Diamond asked, crinkling her face in confusion.

"Diamond, what are you smoking these days? You can't follow me?" I said out of frustration. "Have you heard about a missing pregnant girl that was found dead over on Highway 3? It's all over the news. Have you watched TV lately?"

"Hell no, I ain't seen or heard nothing about no missing girl or baby! Bitch, you know I don't watch the news!" Diamond exclaimed. "C'mon now, I'm a fucking lady of the night, when do I have time to watch news about shit that ain't got nothing to do with me!"

I knew that, but I thought I would throw it out there. More and more I was realizing just how much of a fucking mess my friend was.

"Well, I seen this girl right here on the news!" I said, snatching the picture from her this time and putting it close to her eyes. "Same face . . . same girl. Now put that together with the fact I heard Duke telling that Dr. Gavin to make sure he gets these babies no matter what . . . and what do you have?"

Diamond looked as if she was concentrating. "That's some shit," Diamond replied.

I had finally gotten through to her.

"I started to turn over the pictures and the information I stole from Duke's condo to the police. But you know what? I said, why not get something out of this shit. So I decided I will put the screws to Duke's ass. I'm going to threaten him with going to the media and the police with what I know if he don't give me some serious paper. This nigga just thought he could take everything I had, leave me with nothing and get married on me without any consequences? Hell no, it ain't going down like that."

Diamond was all ears. I knew anything that had to do with money she would be down for it. Once I was sure I had her undivided attention, I told her what I needed.

"So I need your help with putting together a solid plan where I can get the money from his ass safely and get the fuck outta dodge. Of course I'ma hit you off with your share for any help you give me with this," I told her. I was saying the key words and Diamond was into it.

"So, here's what I had in mind for us to do," I continued. "Maybe we can—"

Before I could brainstorm some of my ideas about the blackmail plan, this muthafucka, Brian, knocked on my bedroom door.

"Diamond!" the worthless asshole yelled from the other side of the door.

I instantly cut my words short. I didn't want him to hear anything about my plans. Not only did I not like Brian, I didn't trust him as far as I could throw his ass.

"What?" Diamond responded. She stood up and I knew that meant our meeting was over.

"Bring your ass out here before we have problems!" he barked. "You think a nigga got time to be sitting in your room alone playing with my dick! I came here to see you, now get the fuck out here before I bounce on your dumb ass."

I couldn't believe how disrespectful this nigga was towards Diamond. It seemed as if she would just accept anything from his ass and for the life of me I could never understand it.

"I'm sorry, girl. Let me go see what this pain in the ass wants," Diamond whispered. It was as if she wasn't even embarrassed by Brian's rude displays. I rolled my eyes at her because I was fucking disgusted that she refused to put her damn foot down with him.

"I know, don't mind him," Diamond consoled when she saw how mad I was now. I didn't say a word. "Listen, hold those thoughts about the plans. I'm down for whatever and we can talk all about it in private when I get home from the club tonight."

I softened my face a little bit. Primarily because what other choice did I have. Reluctantly, I agreed to wait for her to talk more about it. There was no way I could do something as serious as this without Diamond. She was way more street savvy than me. She also had her ear to the ground in the streets so putting together a plan would be easy for her.

I sighed loudly and just accepted the fact that I would have no choice but to wait on her. Diamond left out of my room and I could hear her and Brian going at it. I didn't know if they were arguing or fucking again. I closed my eyes and tried to think positive thoughts. I got a little excited about the possibilities of getting my hands on some money.

Together, Diamond and I were going to come up with what I deemed my "cheaper to keep her plan" against Duke.

And I couldn't wait!

Chapter 25

Do or Die

Being in the house with so many thoughts and different variations of plans in my head was driving me crazy.

The anxiety I was feeling was enough to kill me. Not only did I need Diamond to hurry up and come home, I also felt as if I needed a stiff drink to ease my mind. I tried to be patient and wait for Diamond to come home from the club, but it seemed as if I had been waiting for her for days instead of hours. With no real money of my own and nothing to do, I was restless as hell. That was probably the reason I kept obsessing about my plot against Duke. I couldn't wait any longer. I needed to get with Diamond so we could come up with a good plan.

"I can't take this shit no more," I huffed as I started putting on some clothes. I dumped out my purse and counted up the little left over dollar bills and change I had scattered in the bottom of my bag. I counted it, hoping I had enough. *Damn, just made it,* I thought.

I used my last few dollars and called a cab. I had the cabdriver take me to the Magic City. Diamond was going to have to see me now. It was just that serious with me . . . or I was that impatient. I needed to discuss this shit with Diamond and I wasn't confident she would bring her ass home before I conked out or something. She had been keeping some fucked up hours lately. She had also been drinking a lot too. She probably had already forgotten that she promised to come straight home. In any case, I was at the club now so she had no choice but to get with me on this.

When I walked in the club, I was immediately assailed by the strong smell and thick, hazy smoke from cigarettes and weed. I waved my hand in front of my face realizing that being away from the club for so long I was no longer immune to the scent of it. I could hardly breathe and frankly I wanted to gag. I had my face contorted into a nasty scowl. I didn't know how I used to do it in this ghetto ass place and I still didn't know how Diamond was doing it every night.

As I weaved my way through the tables I recognized some of the same old regulars that were always in the club day in and day out. Nothing much had changed about the place. A few patrons spoke to me and asked if I was coming back to work there. I told them hell no, acting as if I had dumped the club instead of the truth, that Neeko wouldn't hire me back out of fear Duke would try to ruin him. I stopped and spoke to a few patrons that told me they missed the way I mixed my drinks. I listened to them complain a little about the new bartender and I found it quite amusing. Shit, I needed an ego booster.

I finally spotted Diamond after scanning the club a few times with my eyes. I twisted my face into a scowl once again when I spotted her. "Fuck!" I hissed. She was busy, which wasn't good for me. She was giving a patron a lap dance, which meant I was going to have to wait for goodness knows how long before she was done. I didn't care. I walked up on her and her customer. "Diamond!" I screamed over the music.

She stopped her dance for a few seconds and looked at me strangely. She looked like she was high on something.

"I'm gonna be at the bar. When you finish, come see me. We gotta talk as soon as possible," I shouted.

Diamond nodded her head as if she was barely able to keep it up, then she started grinding on the guy's dick again. As high as she looked it gave me an uneasy feeling. When I saw the guy reach under her thong and touch her bare pussy that made me queasy. I always thought the rule of the club for lap dancing was no under the clothes contact. Diamond was getting desperate these days. I couldn't believe she was letting a total stranger put his fingers inside of her pussy like that. I stomped away in total disgust. Plus, I was a little worried about her.

I climbed up on a barstool and ordered a shot of Patron. I was scrutinizing the new bartender and I couldn't front, I was envious as hell. She was really cute and the customers that used to skimp on tips with me seemed to be tipping her well. I was pissed off watching this whack ass chick *try to be me* behind the bar. I was jealous as hell. I turned around and went back to watching Diamond instead of the bartender.

My girl was working hard trying to make a quick buck. It was pretty fucking pathetic the way she had to do all of that for those few little dollars. She was dancing to Gucci Mane's rap song, "Lemonade." I didn't know how Diamond did that shit. She was grinding and popping and straddling the guy. I could see the sweat on her body from where I sat. My girl was working too hard for a small payday from these slimy assholes.

I shook my head and took my shot to the head.

I winced as the tequila went down warm. I watched Diamond some more and knew just why I couldn't do that bullshit stripping and lap dancing. Suddenly, I saw Diamond stop dancing. She jumped up off the guy's lap and I saw her waggling her finger in the guy's face and twisting her neck as if she was arguing with him. "Oh shit," I mumbled with my eyes getting wide. I could tell something was going down. I slowly stepped down off the barstool but I didn't move, I just watched for a minute to see if she was going to be able to handle whatever was going on.

"What's up, nigga? I'm dancing like a muthafucka and you ain't pulled out no fucking money yet!" Diamond yelled, her words slurring. Damn, if I could hear her almost clear across the club with loud music playing I knew she was yelling very loud. I saw the dude stand up and stand toe-to-toe with Diamond. He was taller than her but he was right in her face. That's when I started moving slowly towards them. I wasn't about to sit there and let a nigga put his hands on her.

"Where's my fucking money!" Diamond screamed. Now I could hear her better because I was getting closer. The dude pushed Diamond out of his face roughly and told her he wasn't going to give her shit because her pussy stunk. A group of dirty, broke down ass niggas that was with him starting laughing and clowning Diamond. I made it over to them to pull Diamond away before he did something stupid to her, but I wasn't in time to keep her from doing something to him.

Within a blink of an eye, Diamond grabbed a glass of champagne from the table next to the rude guy and threw the shit right in his face. "Argghh!" the dude screamed out. I could tell his eyes must've been on fire because he hadn't seen that shit coming from her.

"Diamond!" I screamed.

The dude pulled himself together real quick and went after her. "You dirty bitch!" he hollered.

The next thing I knew, he pulled back his huge hand and smacked Diamond so hard she went sailing backwards on her ass and hit the floor.

"You muthafucka!" I screamed, racing over to Diamond to see if she was alright. She was looking a little dazed. That bastard stalked over to us, stood above Diamond and hawked a wad of spit right on her.

"You asshole!" Diamond shouted. She was struggling to get off the floor. "Oh no this bitch ass nigga didn't just spit on me!" She wiped the spit off her body, but before she could go back at the guy, the bouncers had finally made their way over to the commotion.

The big, cock diesel bouncers grabbed and tussled with the dude. The guy's friends tried to go at it with the bouncers, but one of the big men lifted his shirt to display a handgun. Those dudes backed down. I guess they had left their shit outside in their cars. All of the men, including the one Diamond had the beef with were forcefully put the hell out of the club. The bouncers followed them all the way just to make sure they didn't try to come back in with any weapons.

All I could do was shake my fucking head. Maybe it was me. I must've been the bad luck because every time I came to the club some shit jumped off. This gave me more of a reason to put my plan in motion. I needed to get my dough from Duke. I was tired of this shit.

"You alright?" I asked Diamond. I knew she wasn't all right, but what else was I gonna say after that whole scene.

"I'm fucking pissed off! I can't take this bullshit no more. These bastards get worse and worse every day," Diamond said as I walked her towards the stairs that led to the dancer's dressing rooms. I guess her high was completely blown now.

When we got downstairs, I sat on a short stool in front of Diamond's little locker where she kept her outfits. I watched as she cleaned the nasty spit off her and got herself together. I took this opportunity to sell my idea. This couldn't have been a better time, because I could tell Diamond was feeling as if she was at the end of her rope.

"See Diamond, you gotta get the fuck up outta this place. This shit is fine for a temporary gig, but long term ain't the move."

Diamond rolled her eyes. "Lynise, I ain't up for no goody two shoes lecture tonight," Diamond snarled at me. "Especially when I'm the bitch footing the bills right now."

"I'm not trying to lecture you," I clarified. "I'm trying to tell you about a plan for both of us to come off with some real money. I had started to tell you about it earlier today before your man interrupted."

Diamond pulled off her skimpy outfit and started putting on her regular clothes. "I'm listening," she said.

"I'm going to blackmail Duke with those pictures and that paperwork. But I need you to be down with this. I need you to help me set up a drop for the money and have my back when it goes down." It was obvious my announcement had caught Diamond slightly off guard.

Diamond looked at me skeptically, but she didn't speak against the plan. I think deep down inside she knew I was on to something. "I'm listening," she said in a low voice. Yes! I, at least, had her ear and her interest now.

"I'm gonna call that nigga and tell him if he don't come up with at least a half-a-mil, I'm going straight to the cops with the information I have about that girl and that fucking butcher shop shelter he running with that doctor," I said.

She looked at me like I had lost my mind. "Bitch, you really think that man is gonna just turn over a half-a-mil just like that? Five hundred thousand dollars for some pictures you got that you can't even prove came from him? C'mon Lynise," Diamond retorted.

"See, that's where you wrong at," I replied. "The paper-work I got has money amounts paid to Duke directly. Yeah, I know it may sound like he was stupid for keeping tabs, but remember he just didn't figure I would ever search his shit."

"If you say so. So you just gon' dial his number, say give me a half-a-mil or else?" Diamond asked with doubt lacing her words.

"Hell yeah!" I replied. "Duke had a lot to lose, Diamond. Without his reputation he won't be able to make no money and if he goes to jail, even worse."

"I hear that hot shit. All of a sudden you a ride or die bitch, huh?" Diamond said sarcastically.

She was starting to piss me off, but I really needed her so I was taking her shit. "It's either ride or die or be broke and fucked up," I replied.

"I don't believe you gonna call him Lynise. It's just not your style . . . maybe my style, but definitely not your corn-ball ass style," Diamond said, twisting her lips. She was egging me by doubting me. Maybe that was a good thing because I needed somebody to hype me up and give me the courage to do this.

"Watch me!" I snapped. "But after I make the call, we need to come up with a quick plan on how to get the money. We need to plot out the where, when and how."

"That's all good . . . that's if you make the call," she said, continuing to doubt me.

Diamond twisted her lips and dared me to make the call. She actually started laughing, saying I wasn't going to make the call.

"A'ight, you don't believe me? I can show you better than I can tell you," I said, snatching Diamond's cell. "Now gimme your phone because he will recognize my number and he won't answer it."

Diamond crossed her arms and watched me closely while I made the call.

I guess she wasn't doubting my seriousness now.

CHAPTER 26

THREAT

Diamond had put the battery in my back, but she wasn't able to soothe my nerves one bit while I made the call.

My heart was hammering when I heard Duke's phone ringing on the other end. I started walking in circles in the dressing room, because I was so damn nervous. Diamond had her arms folded across her chest looking at me like she thought I was faking the call.

"Yeah," Duke answered. I almost shit on myself and cried at the same time when I heard his sexy ass voice. "Speak," Duke called into the phone when I didn't say anything right away.

My mouth was open but nothing was coming out. I was at a loss for words for a minute. Then I heard Duke's fucking wife's voice in the background ask, "Baby, who is that?" That's when I was finally spurned into action. I got angry and that made me feel bold.

"Yeah muthafucka, I'm just calling to tell you that you're done! I have you by the balls and if you don't meet my fucking demands your life is over!" I boomed into the phone.

"What? Who is this? Lynise?" Duke asked nice and calm. I could hear his wife saying something but I couldn't make out what she was saying.

"You damn right it's me!" I hollered into the phone. "I ain't calling to beg for you back or no shit like that, so don't flatter yourself. But I am calling to let you know that your life will be over. I'm calling to tell you that I know all about your little baby snatching ring!"

Duke coughed. It sounded like a nervous cough to me. I was feeling slightly powerful as I spoke. I felt like I had his ass under pressure now. He didn't say anything so I took that as my cue to keep going.

"Oh yeah, I overheard you and Dr. Gavin talking about how ya'll snatch homeless pregnant girls and take their babies by forceful C-section. Then you tell those poor girls that their babies died. That is, if the girls make it . . . see, I saw one of the girls dead on the news. You know just who the fuck I'm talking about too! I also heard you say how many clients is paying you. I also know the babies you said died are actually alive and in the possession of some very rich people. I just so happen to have the list and price you was paid from those people. Oh Duke, I know everything . . . and guess what? I got the pictures Dr. Gavin gave you of all the girls!"

I was telling it all. I wanted him to know how serious the situation was. Duke was quiet and that made me wanna say even more.

"I know one of the girls died from the botched C-section Dr. Gavin gave her at your request. I got the pictures right out of your desk! I can send the cops to the people who bought that baby and when the DNA from the baby matches the dead girl's and I show this list of the people that paid you for that baby, you will be done! Do you hear me done!"

He was listening intently. I could tell. I felt as if I had him right where I wanted him, because if I didn't have his ass in a crunch, knowing Duke like I did, he would have hung up on me a long time ago. Diamond was moving in front of me excitedly trying to ask me what he was saying. I put my hand up halting her while I finished.

"What do you want?" Duke said calmly.

"Now be patient! I was going to tell you," I said with my voice shaking. "Here is what the fuck I want! I want five hundred thousand dollars in cash. I want you to come to the Magic City and bring the shit in a duffel bag. You need to come at a time when the club is packed. I want you to leave the fucking bag on the left side of the bar. You won't see me, but I will see you."

There was silence on the phone. That shit was making me uncomfortable. I mean, here I was extorting his ass and Duke was still cool, calm and collected.

I was kind of shocked at his reaction given the fact he and I both knew my evidence against him was rock solid. "Do you hear me you asshole!" I screamed.

Duke was getting a rise out of me by being so calm. I wanted to get under his skin like he had done to me for so long.

"Ok, Lynise, I will meet your demands," he finally replied. "I will come tomorrow at ten o'clock. Is that good enough for you?"

I felt a flash of heat come over me. It was a combination of excitement and fear. I couldn't believe it was that easy to get him to bring me that kind of money. Something about that didn't sit right with me, but I wasn't going to back down at this point. What if Duke was really willing to pay to have those pictures back? I mean, I had watched him waste large amounts of money before so I already knew money was no object for him.

"You need to follow my instructions and don't try no bullshit. If shit doesn't go down right, I have instructed someone to drop the pictures and stuff off to the cops and the media. I'm sure you don't want your little preacher's daughter wife to be embarrassed publicly when she finds out her so-called Christian husband is a murderer and baby snatcher."

"That is fine. I just need to know who else has been able to review these documents?" Duke asked, sounding all official and strictly business and shit. He was speaking to me like I was some business partner. I guess he didn't want his wife to be suspicious.

"Don't worry about who else knows. You don't know the person. But trust me, if one hair on my head is harmed, the person will turn your ass in so fast you won't know your own name before it hits the general public and every media outlet you can think of," I bluffed. By now Diamond couldn't take not knowing what was going on, so she pressed her ear close to mine and the phone.

"I will be there tomorrow . . . but you need to hand over the documents and pictures when I leave the bag," Duke demanded. I knew he would ask for the stuff, but I was not planning on letting him see me. I was too scared he might try some shit.

"I will leave them in a place that is secure," I replied. "There will be a note in the spot where you will leave the money. When I have seen the money for sure, you will get the information."

There was no fucking way I was going to let him see me. I was going to have Diamond dress in a disguise and pick up the bag when he leaves it.

"Ok, Lynise, I look forward to doing business with you again," Duke said calmly, still sounding all official.

His demeanor unnerved me. It was strange for someone being blackmailed to be this calm. Diamond moved her head away from the phone and looked at me. After I hung up the phone, I was completely spooked. My hands were trembling and sweat was pouring down my back.

"What happened at the end of the conversation?" Diamond asked. Damn, she seemed nervous too. Shit, I didn't know if we could survive this. Hope was becoming my best friend.

"He said he was going to do it tomorrow at ten," I told her. "But he was too fucking calm, girl. It was real weird he was that damn calm."

Diamond was quiet and so was I. Both of our minds were racing. I could tell. I was biting on my nails to try and combat the huge butterflies flitting around in my stomach.

"Girl, that shit just didn't seem right. It was just way too easy. I'm scared as hell now," I admitted. I paced up and down the little cramped dressing room.

"Your ass wanna get spooked after the threat!" Diamond chastised.

"Girl, this is all gonna be behind us tomorrow," I tried to convince her. I was really trying to convince myself.

"You really think a man like Duke is just gonna hand over that kind of money after being strong armed by you?" Diamond asked. She was playing with her hair. I knew that meant she was nervous as hell too.

"Yup! Because he knows I'm telling the fucking truth about his misdeeds. He also knows now that I have his client list and if the cops investigate and go check up on those babies, a whole lot of shit gonna hit the fan."

"Well, what you gonna do in the meantime?"

"I don't' think I should go to the apartment that's for sure," I answered. "I can't be sure that he won't come there and try some shit. I don't have any cash, but if you loan me a hundred dollars I'll get a place to stay for the night."

Diamond sighed loudly. "Where you gonna stay at for a hundred dollars?" she asked.

"Any of the hotels down Virginia Beach. I just wanna lay low until it goes down and I'm free and clear. Just think, after tomorrow I won't need to borrow a hundred damn dollars and you won't need to shake your ass for dirty niggas like that one tonight." I smiled after my statement. We both needed to chill. This day was the worst and the calm and coolness of Mr. Duke Carrington had us both shaking in our boots.

"Very fucking true girl!" Diamond shouted happily.

With that, Diamond dug in her purse and handed me a wad of dollars and fives. I counted out a hundred and handed her back the extra.

"Bitch, when you get this money from Duke, you better give me ten times a hundred!" Diamond joked.

"Oh, hell yeah, you know I will hook you up," I said, feeling slightly better. "Girl, you can get like a hundred thousand, shit. My only condition is that you keep your damn mouth shut about where the money came from and don't spend it for a while. I mean, you can't even tell Brian about this shit."

Diamond sucked her teeth as if I had insulted her. Hell, she knew I was serious. And I hoped I hadn't fucked up by telling Diamond. Once reliable, now she suffered from diarrhea of the mouth.

"C'mon now, you know damn well I don't run my mouth like that!" she snapped.

Yeah, the old drug-free you didn't normally run your mouth, but the new always high Diamond suffered from the disease called loose lips, I thought to myself. Thoughts I kept to myself.

"You want me to drop you off at a hotel?" she asked.

"Yeah, and after that I want you to go in the house and stay inside until you come to the club tomorrow. Duke never knew what apartment we were in, so if you're inside, you will be safe."

"True. Then tomorrow I will get Brian to walk me out . . . you know, just in case the crazy nigga shows up," Diamond assured me.

"I hate Brian but that's a damn good idea," I concluded.

Diamond and I left the club together through the alleyway back door with thoughts of big money on our minds. As we left, I thought how perfect that little back door was for my escape when I got the money from Duke. Instead of going out the front door and risking him doing some foul shit, I would make a run for the back door, which I'm sure he probably knew nothing about. As Diamond rambled on, I even thought about where I was going to park her car for the getaway too. I would park way down in the alley that the back door led to. Before Duke realized I wasn't coming out the front and started searching for me, I'd be long gone.

After we left the club, Diamond dropped me off at the Doubletree Hotel at the Military Circle Mall. Before I got out of her car, we hugged each other and agreed to see each other tomorrow. I had asked Diamond several times if she thought she should stay with me at the hotel and not return to our apartment. She was adamant that she needed to meet up with Brian.

I was uneasy, but I went along with her wishes. I hoped all went according to plan and she'd be safe. "Bye," Diamond said to me as I exited her car.

"Bye is permanent, girl. Let's just say see you later," I corrected her.

At that moment, a *rush* came over me. I didn't know why or what it was all about. Something about the word *bye* spoke of finality. I was so hoping it was just a funny feeling. After all, it was the end of a long day.

Diamond laughed. "Ok, see you later Nini. Is that better?"

I smiled. I so loved her laugh. "Yes, because saying *bye* means I won't ever see you again," I told her.

I just didn't know how prophetic my words would be.

Chapter 27

On A Mission

I rushed into the Doubletree and paid for one night. The clerk tried to give me a hard time because I was paying with cash. And the Doubletree similar to most hotels required a credit card. I came up with a quick but viable lie about my bag being stolen. I flashed him a smile or two and finally, he folded and gave me a room for cash. I even got his ass to use his employee discount to book my room at a cheaper rate.

Inside the room, I used the little notepad to sketch out the inside of the *Magic City*. I wanted a visual of where Duke would leave the money, how I would get Diamond to pick it up and more importantly, how we were going to get the fuck out of there and get away. I reviewed my sketch and went over my plan at a hundred times.

I finally felt drowsy. Lying down, I thought sleep was calling my name. I was wrong. I had a hard time sleeping in the hotel room. Every little noise, creak or voice outside of my door woke me up. I must've got up more than ten times during the night. I watched TV for a few minutes, paced the length of the room, looked out the window, laid back down and then repeated the process of trying to sleep all over again. A few times I drifted into a fitful sleep, but never a deep enough sleep to feel rested.

When the sun finally streamed through the windows of the hotel room, I decided to get up and call Diamond. I had been worried about her all night. Another reason for my restlessness. I should have insisted on her staying with me last night. I hadn't wanted her to go back to the apartment for fear of any retaliation Duke might be planning. But Diamond had insisted she'd be alright. I picked up my cell and called Diamond's phone. It just rang. I knew it was early, but at a time such as this, her ass supposed to answer. I had told her to make sure anytime I called her that she picked up her damn phone.

I took a deep breath and called her again. Still no answer. "C'mon Diamond, this ain't no time to be playing disappearing acts and shit," I cursed out loud as I dialed her number three more times in succession.

No answer.

I had a sick feeling in the pit of my stomach now. I told myself to calm down. I convinced myself that Diamond was just sleeping after a hard night's work at the club. I threw my phone on the bed and stood still for a minute. I was starting to doubt myself with this plan.

"Maybe I should've just tried to get what I could with the bank information I had kept." I was doing it again—talking to myself, thinking out loud. Nervousness kicking my ass. I had contemplated trying to get what I could a few times, but I had also called and fucked up all of Duke's bank accounts. I was sure he had straightened out by now . . . which also meant that there was probably a serious fraud watch on.

"Fuck!" I cursed out of frustration. I needed to calm down.

I walked into the bathroom and decided I needed a hot shower. Then I would order some room service to kill time until I heard back from Diamond. I was going to let more time pass before I tried to call her again. I got into the steamy shower and let the water cascade down my body. I closed my eyes and let my mind drift to good thoughts. I fantasized about what I was going to do with the money that I was about to get from shaking Duke's ass down. I knew one of the first things I was going to do was get the hell out of Virginia.

There were too many memories in Virginia Beach for me.

I wanted bigger and better for myself. I had always wanted to live on the west coast. Maybe California . . . the land of the beautiful people. I found myself smiling as I envisioned myself in L.A., bartending at some of the most upscale celebrity clubs where I would get tips so big, I could shop every day.

I would probably live right down in Beverly Hills someplace. My apartment would be small, but swanky and upscale. I was smiling in the shower and I realized it when some of the water got into my mouth. I wiped my face and with that I wiped the fantasy from my mind.

"Get the money first," I whispered to myself.

When I did get my hands on the money, my intention was to start from scratch. I wanted a fresh start, a new beginning. I was going to put all of my hurt and broken heartedness behind me. I was feeling good about my decision to blackmail and extort Duke now.

When I got out of the shower, I slipped into the same clothes I had worn the night before. I hadn't had time to go back to the apartment or anywhere else to get any accessories. I picked up the phone and dialed Diamond again.

Still no answer.

"This chick is playing herself!" I mumbled in a harsh whisper. "Why wouldn't you answer your damn phone knowing I was going to be fucking worried about you, Diamond!" I yelled out as if she was on the phone.

I was starting to get scared as hell now and I had no way to leave the fucking hotel. I told that trifling bitch she would have to come and get me. We were planning to lay low until ten o'clock when Duke was to drop off the fucking money. *Now what?* She was nowhere to be found. I mean if she was with Brian the least she could've done was call me and tell me she was alive. I knew that nigga, Brian, kept her under lock and key when he was around, but damn, she knew how important staying in constant communication with me was. We had talked about this the entire ride to the hotel the night before.

I unfolded the few dollars I had left of the money Diamond had loaned me for the hotel room. It was a good thing the clerk had given me a discount or else I wouldn't have had anything leftover. Even with that act of generosity, I was pissed I only had twenty dollars. That wasn't enough for another night and it was barely enough to take a cab from the hotel to the club.

I walked in circles trying to decide what I was going to do. I couldn't believe Diamond had let me down like this. With all of this money on the line, she was doing one of her dumb ass disappearing acts. I sat on the edge of the bed and put my head in my hands, still praying that I would hear from her at any minute.

I noticed the hotel had slid my check-out receipt under the door. That meant I had to get the hell out of the hotel within the next hour. I didn't have a choice. I was going to have to catch a cab back to my apartment. That was the only place I could afford to go with the amount of money I had leftover. I could only pray Duke wasn't sitting on the complex, lying in wait to mug my ass.

Five more calls to Diamond rendered the same results. With no other choice, I checked out of the hotel. I had the front desk clerk call me a cab and with a knot the size of a watermelon growing in my stomach, I went back to my apartment looking for Diamond. When the taxi pulled up to my complex, I scanned the area suspiciously, looking for any strange cars. I didn't notice anything unusual. I had also noticed that Diamond's car wasn't parked outside the apartment.

"This bitch done left without calling me or anything," I mumbled as I handed the cab driver my last few dollars. I rushed out of the cab and ran up the stairs to my apartment. I quickly went inside and once in, I felt safe. "Diamond!" I called out just to make sure. There was no answer. I was fuming mad now. Anything could've happened. I called her cell phone again. This time I got an answer.

"Hello?" I said, crinkling my eyebrows, ready to lay in on Diamond for being missing in action. But the line quickly went dead. I swear I could've fainted. That's how nervous I got all of a sudden. I looked at the phone strangely. Immediately, my instincts told me something wasn't right. I went through the apartment pulling all the shades down and making sure the door was double locked. Suddenly, my phone rang back in my hand. That shit caused me to almost jump out of my skin. I looked down at the screen and Diamond's name and number was flashing.

"Ok, she's calling back. Maybe I'm just being crazy," I said to myself in a lumber voice. Damn, I was relieved. After I curse her ass out, I was going to have a good laugh at how nervous and scared I was.

I answered the phone to tell her ass off. "Diamond?" I huffed into the receiver with much attitude.

"If you ever want to see Diamond again, you will do everything you're told to do," a voice said into the phone. It sounded like the person was using a computerized voice. A hot feeling flashed in my chest and my heart started running wild. I felt vomit creeping up my throat.

"Who is this!" I screamed, my voice cracking.

The next thing I heard gave me a sharp stabbing pain in my chest.

"Lynise! Please do what they say! Help me! Don't let me die!" I heard Diamond boom through the phone in a bloodcurdling scream.

I cupped my hand over my mouth. She sounded as if she was in a lot of pain.

"Was that enough of a warning for you? If not, we can continue to send you those types of calls," the mechanical voice told me.

My legs got weak and I fell to my knees in the middle of the living room floor. I cried and couldn't even speak. I had put Diamond in harm's way. This was definitely all my fault. Duke was going to kill her now.

How could I have been so stupid and so selfish?

"What do you want from me," I managed to say through my tears. At this point, I felt like I'd truly do anything to get my friend back. No amount of money was worth her life.

"You will be contacted again with instructions. If you fail to do everything we say, or if you try to go to the police, your friend will die and you will be next," the computer-generated voice threatened.

The tears fell from my eyes even harder.

189 | CHEAPER *to* KEEP HER

Once again, I had been bested by Duke Carrington.
At least for now.

CHAPTER 28
A DIAMOND IS FOREVER

After the call I had a pounding headache.

Understandably I felt like shit. I had let my best friend down. I could only hope and pray Duke didn't kill her. Of course that was a stupid thought on my part. All the shit he had done and I was blind to how ruthless Duke Carrington really was. I loved a relentless, ruthless fool who was more criminal than businessman. And now, that fact finally hit me and didn't escape me. He had the acumen of a crude businessman coupled with the undying coldness of a ruthless criminal. *A deadly damn combination.*

I was truly lost for a solution. Waiting was all I could do and it was absolutely killing me inside. I had been up almost twenty-four hours waiting to hear back from Duke and his little goons that had kidnapped Diamond. I had cried until I was literally out of tears. I had also tried to call Diamond's phone back several times but it was going straight to voice-mail, which left me with an ominous feeling in the pit of my stomach. I figured maybe reasoning with Duke was what I needed to do. If he had agreed to just let Diamond go, I would give him his shit back and call it fair. That was a big fucking pipe dream. I knew Duke didn't want to hear anything from me at this point.

I had fucked up. I couldn't let sleeping dogs die . . . now my best friend was going to die for my selfishness and pride.

As I waited to hear back from them, Brian showed up at the apartment. He came in with a key and scared the shit out of me. He didn't speak because that's just how things were between him and me. He headed straight for Diamond's room.

"She's not in there," I called out to him. I had no choice but to put my differences aside and speak to Brian. I busted out crying. Brian came back in the living room and looked at me strangely.

"What's up?" he asked, his face in a scowl.

Inside, I was scared as shit. As much as I despise this man, he was the love of Diamond's life and I was the reason they may not ever be together again. But I had to woman up.

"Somebody got Diamond!" I blurted out. It felt real good to tell somebody about what was going on. I needed to get it off my chest. I was very happy to see Brian for the first time since we'd met.

"What the fuck you mean somebody got Diamond?" he asked with much attitude. He disliked me just as much I did him. I swallowed hard when he yelled at me.

"Me and Diamond was gonna . . . well . . . I was gonna," I tried to get the words out but they were stuck. I couldn't speak or look at Brian. He grabbed me by my shoulders and shook me hard. That made me cry even harder.

"What the fuck is you trying to say Lynise? What the fuck you talking 'bout right now?" he urged, shaking my shoulders frantically. I was crying so hard I was hyperventilating. Brian pushed me down on the couch so I could try to calm down.

"Yo, I'm fucking listening!" he growled, standing over me as he waited for an answer.

I inhaled deeply and steadied my voice. "They took Diamond because . . . because . . . I was going to blackmail my ex. He killed this girl and I have proof, so me and Diamond was gonna pick up some money tonight and I was gonna give Diamond some of it. But I told her not to stay here by herself last night. I just don't know what happened! I don't know how they got her! I'm sorry!" I was rambling like a fool and I knew Brian couldn't make heads nor tails about what I was talking about.

Between my tears, I told Brian more about what was going on. Afterwards, I cried some more. The tears wouldn't stop.

"Yo, who is it? I will murder a nigga right now!" Brian gritted, moving around the room as if he could kill somebody right then and there.

"No! You can't go after them or go to the cops or they said they will kill her!" I pleaded frantically.

"How they gon' know? I'm saying they got my girl, what the fuck I'm supposed to do, just sit around here and do shit," he huffed.

I was shaking my head left to right. I had to make Brian understand just how serious this was. He couldn't play tough guy in this situation.

"I have to wait until they call me and tell me what to do next. I'm sure they want the pictures and the paperwork back. I think once I give it back they will let Diamond go. Fuck the money." Honestly, I didn't know if they even wanted the pictures back or if they were just going to kill Diamond to teach me a lesson.

"You really think it's gon' be that easy? If they real niggas, they ain't just gon' let her go like that!" Brian screamed on me. "I'ma call her phone," he said defiantly.

"No, please Brian! Give them a chance to call me because if they think I told you they might hurt her," I begged him.

I could see him thinking. That was a good thing.

"Fuck!" Brian screamed, throwing his own cell phone against the wall. That was exactly how I felt as well. Brian and I sat in silence for the next two hours. He would get up, peep out the window and come back and sit down again. I was so tired my insides hurt, but I refused to go to sleep for fear that I'd miss their call or Brian would call and make things worse.

I got up to use the bathroom and that was when I noticed something sticking under the door. I walked over, picked it up and examined it. It was a manila envelope. The handwriting was horrible but readable:

A DIAMOND IS FOREVER.

I clutched it tightly. Somebody had come right to the fucking apartment door, which caused a chill to shoot down my spine. "Brian," I said quietly, barely audible. I waved the envelope in my trembling hands.

He rushed over to me and snatched the envelope from me. I pointed to the door to alert him where it had come from. Brian pulled a pistol out of his waistband and rushed to the door. He snatched it open and peeped outside. Then he stepped out and whirled around with his gun in his hands.

"Fucking cowards!" he hollered and came back into the apartment. He ripped open the envelope and slid out the contents.

"Awww!" Brian cried out when he examined the contents. I put my hands over my mouth and the tears flowed in buckets once again. I could see it was pictures in Brian's hand. I could tell by his face it wasn't good. I snatched the pictures and looked at them. No lie, I swear I felt my heart seize. A tight feeling came over my entire body and I imagined that's what people who had heart attacks felt like.

"Aggghhhh!" I screamed, dropping the pictures onto the floor as if they had burned me or something. I looked down at them again through tear-filled eyes. Diamond was naked and tied to a chair. Her face was completely covered with blood and I could tell her hair had been haphazardly cut. One of the pictures was a close up of the blood on her face and the cuts and bruises on her body. It looked as if they had been beating her for days, instead of hours. I knew I had to act fast. From the looks of it, there was no way Diamond could withstand much more of what they had already done to her.

"Ohhhh, Diamond!" I cried out. "I'm so sorry I got you into this."

Before I could say another word, my cell phone rang. It was Diamond's cell. I showed the screen to Brian and told him to be quiet by putting my finger up against my lips.

"Hello?" I gulped, swallowing back tears and snot.

"I guess you and your company know we're serious now, huh?" the computer-generated voice stated.

"Please! Take me. She has nothing to do with this," I pleaded.

"It's too late to think about that now. You have twenty minutes to get to the women's homeless shelter. I'm sure you know which one, since you seem to know a lot. You need to be alone. There will be two pregnant girls in the front. They have something for you. Pick it up and wait for further instructions." The line went dead.

I looked at Brian, my eyes filled with tears. I didn't even think about the fact they knew he was there.

I was fully focused on following their instructions to get Diamond out of this.

CHAPTER 29
IF I SHOULD DIE

I practically argued with Brian convincing him he couldn't go to the woman's homeless shelter.

He didn't want to listen to reason. He was ready to go wherever with guns blazing.

"Do you want her to die without even letting me try to get her released?" I screamed at him.

Finally, after about ten minutes of arguing I was able to get through to his stubborn ass. I was confident if they saw him with me they would do something even crazier to Diamond. Brian told me I could use his car to go to the shelter. He told he was going to have one of his boys pick him up and he would meet me back at the apartment later. All the time I spent hating him, I was now happy to have his ass around. Brian was like a man apart when he found out about what was going on with Diamond.

Maybe he did actually love her.

I took his keys and we left the apartment together. He walked me to his car and told me to call him as soon I could.

"Brian, if I should d-d-d-die," I paused. Just the thought sent chills through my body. "What they want is in my room. It's hidden real good. You'll find it eventually if you look."

He nodded and I got into his car. I began backing out of the parking spot and left Brian standing on the curb waiting for his friend to pick him up. I looked down at the stick shift to put the car into drive when suddenly I heard a BOOM BOOM! Two loud cannon sounding shots explored in the parking lot. I jumped fiercely.

I grew up in the hook. I knew the sound of guns. This was the real deal. These shots sounded close. My eyes went as wide as marbles when I saw Brian's body shrink to the ground. He was laid out in front of his car on the concrete.

"Oh my God!" I screamed. I started shaking all over again. Barely able to catch my breath, I wheeled the car around and the tires started screeching. I was trying to get the fuck out of there. I sped out of the parking lot like a mad woman and as I eased onto the highway my phone started ringing again. I was scared as hell to answer it. But I was also scared of what might happen if I didn't answer it. I reached down and picked it up, keeping my other hand on the steering wheel.

"You just had an innocent person killed," the same computerized voice said. "Matter of fact, you were the one to kill him. Now I guess you will listen to the instructions you are given."

I just sobbed into the phone. I couldn't speak. I was damaged. I was a bitch. I was a complete fuck up. If I could rewind back to the day I met Duke, I would just walk away and don't fall for the *hokey doke*. It was the same *hokey doke* that had gotten my best friend's beaten and possibly killed and her boyfriend shot.

I had gotten myself and Diamond into this shit. It was up to me to get us out of this shit.

I drove like a bat out of hell to the shelter as I was instructed to do. When I got there, I saw the two pregnant girls the voice said would be there standing outside. Then the phone rang again. I answered right away.

"Put them both in the car and drive them around the block two times and then bring them back," the irritating computer-generated voice commanded me. "No matter what you have to do to get them in the car, you better do it. Diamond's life depends on it."

Even though the voice was disguised, it still came across as pure evil. *What the fuck kind of crazy demands is this bastard giving me now!* I thought to myself. I put the car in park and got out. I walked up to the girls and told them they needed to come with me. One girl handed me an envelope and looked as if she was scared to death because when she extended her hand with the envelope it was very unsteady from shaking so badly.

Both girls were very big and obviously far gone in their pregnancies. "Ya'll have to come with me in the car," I said to them. One girl started to cry as if on cue. I looked at this bitch as if she was crazy.

"I'm not going! No . . . please! I can't go through that again! Please just leave me alone!" she cried out.

I was shocked by her reaction, but I had a mission to complete and if I had to fuck this little girl up, I was prepared to do it.

"Look, I'm not trying to hurt you, but if you don't get in this fucking car, something is going to happen to my friend.

I'm not about to let that shit happen so I'm asking you to just get your ass in the car!" I told the girl forcefully.

She wouldn't budge. I grabbed that bitch by arm and started pulling her.

"No! Please!" she screamed at the top of her lungs.

"Why the fuck are you acting crazy?" I screamed, dragging her forward.

She was resisting as if she thought I was taking her to a slaughterhouse. Maybe she did think that, judging by what Duke and Dr. Gavin had going on. The other girl started crying too but she was going towards the car on her own, although reluctantly.

"Why are ya'll crying? I don't know what they told you about me but I'm not down with them! Now, just make this shit easy and get the fuck in the car!" I gritted on these bitches.

I was sweating now. I began pulling that bitch with all my might. Finally, she started dragging her feet towards the car. She got in. Once I was back behind the steering wheel, I drove around the block twice like I had been instructed to do. Then I got another call telling me to drop both of the girls back off at the shelter, but this time at the back door. When I pulled back up, two big strapping men came and grabbed the girls out of the car. The girls were screaming again, even worse than before. I felt horrible inside. One of the men came over to the window and handed me another envelope that looked similar to the one that was slid under the door.

My heart skipped a beat. The last time I opened an envelope I saw pictures of Diamond. *What the fuck is it now?* I thought to myself. I ripped it open and pulled out more pictures. I stared at the images and banged my fists on the steering wheel. I was finally able to figure out what they were trying to do now. The tables had been turned.

This time the finger was pointing directly at me.

The phone rang again. I wanted to take that shit and throw it out of the window. Instead, I thought about Diamond and I hesitantly picked up the phone.

"How do you like seeing yourself kidnapping young, homeless pregnant girls?" the computerized voice asked. I just closed my eyes. These muthafuckas were playing hard-ball now.

"Two can play your game. So I guess we have to arrange for you to turn over the pictures and documents back to us. When you do that, you can have the images of yourself, you can get your best friend back, and you can be cleared of murdering her boyfriend."

"When can we do this meeting? I just want out of this," I cried into the phone.

The computerized voice laughed. The computer device made the laugh sound shrilled in my soul and it unnerved me. "I find that funny. Now you don't want to play the blackmail game anymore?"

I bit down into my jaw and put my head down on the steering wheel. I just wanted my life back, the life of a low paid bartender trying to get ahead. The simple life I had before I ever met Duke Carrington. A life I would never complain about again.

"No, I just want to move on . . . everybody just move on and forget this ever happened," I croaked out.

"That will never happen. It's time for new beginnings. Go back to the apartment and wait to hear from us again," the voice instructed.

"Let me speak to Diamond," I demanded, I wanted to know she was still alive before I did anymore of their bullshit biddings. But the phone line went dead. I slammed my fists on the steering wheel again.

This was the first time in a while I had to admit I was in way over my head.

CHAPTER 30

REGRETS

I was both physically and emotionally drained as I drove back to my apartment complex as I had been instructed. When I pulled into the complex, I could barely maneuver the car to a parking spot because of the police and emergency vehicles haphazardly parked all over the area. There was a crowd standing behind a cordoned off area. The crime scene was because of Brian's shooting. I hadn't forgotten about Brian but I was somewhat surprised by the scene. I was so scared to get out of the damn car for fear that whoever shot Brian would shoot my ass too.

"Fuck!" I cursed as I looked around. Here I was pulling the fuck up in a dead man's ride. When I went to get out of the car I noticed a couple of guys I remembered seeing Brian with standing behind the crime scene tape. As soon as they spotted his car, I could see them squinting to see who was pulling up and getting out of Brian's car. They eyed me evilly but didn't say anything or bring any attention to me.

I wanted to tell the police what happened so desperately but I couldn't chance it. I was almost one hundred percent sure that Duke would have somebody out there ready to snipe my ass if I even tried. The cops weren't letting anybody go up the staircase closest to my apartment door. I had to go all the way on the other side of the complex, walk up the far side staircase and walk across the little tiers outside of the apartments in order to get back to my place.

I went inside, bolted my door and went straight to my bedroom. I flopped on my bed and just balled out crying some more. Duke had made me shed some fucking tears over these past few months for sure. I was thinking of all kinds of ways I was going to get revenge on his ass. I just had to get Diamond free first. I lay on my bed waiting for the next call to come.

Every now and then I would get up to see if the police had cleared the crime scene yet. One of the times I was looking out the window, I suddenly heard knocking on the apartment door. I swallowed a lump of fear that had lodged in my throat from the banging. I wasn't trying to answer the damn door. By now, not only was Duke going to be after me, Brian's friends were now wondering for sure what role I played in his murder. It wasn't a secret in Virginia Beach that I despised Brian. But I don't know how they could think I would just murk the nigga for no reason. I'm sure his people didn't want to go to the police on me, because the 'hood had its own set of laws and number one on the list was *no snitching*. They'd rather take care of my ass themselves. They would have to join the growing list of people after me.

Whoever was at the door was banging like crazy now. Honestly, I was so scared I slid down to the floor and got underneath my bed. I didn't know what else to do. I felt as if I was caught up in a horror movie. Eventually, the person stopped banging. I waited a while, then I rolled out from under the bed and dialed Diamond's phone number. I figured I could speed up the process of arranging a meeting to turn over the damming evidence I had, so I could get Diamond back.

Her phone went straight to voicemail. "Shit!" I cursed. I think the waiting was worse than everything else. I got off the floor and tipped to the window again. There were still police cars outside. Now they had added unmarked cars to the gang of cars already out there. I waited and waited and waited for the next call. But none came. I kept trying to call the phone back but it repeatedly kept going directly to voicemail. I had been so deprived of sleep I finally just conked out on my bed.

I don't know how long I was asleep before I jumped up to loud banging. "Again!" I said groggily as I was jolted out of my sleep. It sounded like a boulder was coming through my apartment. The next sound I heard shocked me so bad, a little bit of piss trickled out of my bladder.

"Police! Don't fucking move!" they screamed. There were at least ten guns pointed at me. I raised my hands up in surrender and in utter and complete shock. I felt like my legs were made of jelly and they threatened to buckled under me.

"Lynise Washington, we have a warrant for your arrest in connection with the murder of Tania Blackmon," one of the cops screamed at me.

Who? Murder? Me? I screamed inside my head. My eyes were blinking a mile a minute. I had no fucking idea what he was talking about. The cop grabbed me up roughly and called a female cop over to search me.

"Start searching the house!" another cop yelled. There was a bunch of them and they started pillaging my apartment. For what, at that time, I had no fucking clue. They were throwing shit around and just tearing up the place. I was led into the living room and made to sit on one of the kitchen chairs that they had dragged over.

"I don't know what this is all about. I think I'm being framed for something I didn't do," I finally said with a shaky voice.

"Yeah, that's what they all say when they get to this point. You're busted," a nasty female cop spat at me. This bitch was ugly as sin. I knew she hated the fact that I looked better than her.

"I didn't fucking do anything. I know who did it! I tried to report what I knew and clear myself once before. I came to the police station with the information I had, but no one would take the time out to listen!" I screamed.

"Uh huh, I'm sure," the cop replied sarcastically.

I couldn't believe this shit. They were going through my apartment with a fine tooth comb. They were tossing shit around and I even heard shit being broken.

"Bingo!" I heard one of the male cops yell from my bedroom. My heart started racing so fast I was beginning to feel lightheaded.

"We got what we call direct physical evidence right fucking here!" the cop announced. "Just like the crime stoppers tipster said we would find it and where . . . we sure did. That fucking tip was right on the money."

He was holding the pictures I had stolen from Duke's condo, along with the paperwork about the baby sales. I almost passed out right where I sat. "Wait . . . no . . . you don't understand!" I screamed defensively.

"Shut the fuck up, you murderous bitch! You and that fucking doctor are done!" the male cop spat.

"I can't believe she was bold enough . . . or stupid enough rather to keep pictures of a girl she had brutally murdered. What a dumb ass!" the female cop commented.

I just lost it at that point. I stood up with my hands cuffed behind my back. I was stumbling and off balance. When I was steady on my two feet, I started jumping up and down screaming as if I was a straight up mental patient. It didn't take long before a few of the cops inside the apartment bum rushed me and threw me down on the floor.

"Take this murderer down to the stationhouse so she can be booked and processed. She disgusts me! We're gonna finish searching here. Then I will get somebody to do her car," I heard the cop say.

My car? I screamed inside of my head. I didn't even have a car. As I was being led out of my apartment to a waiting paddy wagon, I saw that the cops were impounding Brian's car. They thought it was my car and then I remember that the pictures of those girls at the shelter being pulled towards the car were in the car. I was really going to look like a kidnapping, baby snatching murderer now. I had to admit to myself this seemed to be a very well thought out revenge plan on Duke's part.

Inside the paddy wagon I cried and cried. I could only imagine what must've happened to Diamond by now and me going to jail I wouldn't be able to help her. I was in a fucking world of shit and I didn't have a soul to call on. I was having so many regrets as I reflected on the last couple of weeks of my life. I should have just followed my first mind and turned Duke in. Me being greedy and trying to get some money to start a new life was the reason I was in this predicament.

Duke was smarter than I thought. Of course he was. He was a businessman and entrepreneur as well as a criminal mastermind. I had to give him credit for this elaborate scheme. I immediately started to pray. There had to be a way out of this mess.

If so, I had to figure it out and fast!

Chapter 31
Guilty Until Proven Innocent

I was locked up, incarcerated, behind bars. Regardless of how you put it, the shit didn't sound right and definitely didn't seem right. But bottom line, I was really fucking locked up.

After the first night in central cell, I was taken to court and arraigned. I was being charged with murder, kidnapping, assault, illegal adoption enterprise, racketeering, conspiracy and child endangerment. I mean they were fucking trying to throw the book at me for crimes I had nothing to do with.

After central cell, I was transferred to the Virginia Beach Jail for Woman. This was the location women were held prior to their trial or being assigned a permanent prison. I didn't have a trial date yet. Unlike central cell, which included multiple cells with an overflow of women, this location had cellblocks and individual cells that held two to four inmates.

Once I was assigned to a cellblock, shit went haywire. While sleeping one particular afternoon, I was startled out of my sleep by a pillowcase being placed over my head. Additionally, something was covering my nose and mouth, so I couldn't scream. I tried to fight back, but it was too many of them.

"Bitch, you wanna fucking kill babies! You wanna steal people's babies! Fucking bitch!" I wasn't sure, but I think it was multiple women screaming and beating the shit out of me. They kicked and punched my torso, my arms, legs, feet . . . any part of my body they could get to. I felt like my ribs had been cracked and my skull fractured. They beat me until I felt blood seeping through the material they had on my head. Finally, one hard punch to my jaw snapped my head back and my world went black.

I woke up in the jail's infirmary. My entire body ached from head to toe. The nurse told me chicks in jail didn't take kindly to women who harmed babies. I had cried and tried to talk through my wired jaw to tell her I hadn't done the crimes I was being accused of. It was no use. When an inmate said she was innocent, no one ever believed her. *Hell, everyone was innocent in prison.*

I stayed in the infirmary for a couple of weeks before I was finally transferred to a solitary confinement unit, away from the main population. It was for my own safety and not for behavioral reasons like some of the other inmates that had to stay locked in a solitary cell twenty-three hours a day—one hour was given for exercising or stretching your legs.

When I was finally assigned a court appointed attorney, he came to visit me and started telling me about the so-called evidence they had amassed against me. Not only had they taken the pictures and paperwork I had stolen from Duke and used that against me, they had also apparently found a bunch of planted evidence, such as other pictures of me allegedly in the act of running the baby snatching ring, the murder weapon used in Brian's shooting and they claimed they had surveillance of me going in and out of the condo where they claim the illegal business was run out of. Apparently, Dr. Gavin had struck a deal with the prosecutors and he was granted immunity for testimony against me.

This was too much to deal with.

Some days I contemplated just committing suicide. I had pleaded with my attorney to believe me. I told him everything leading up to this, but he maintained that all of the physical evidence in the case pointed towards me. I even told him that whoever had framed me had more than likely killed my best friend. But he said the police hadn't received any missing person reports for Diamond nor had they discovered any bodies. He wouldn't listen to reason for shit.

How did I expect a jury of my peers or a court of law to listen to me? I was fucked . . . and worse, I knew it.

"Ms. Washington, at this point they found so much evidence inside your home that I would suggest you not try to fight this case at trial," my attorney said gravely during one of his visits.

I'm sure his advice came from the fact that he was being paid a low salary from the state of Virginia and not the big bucks defense attorneys with high income clients get paid. It was a well known fact in the 'hood that court appointed attorneys never wanted to go to trial. They got paid the same salary, trial or plea deal.

"I'm not pleading guilty to crimes I didn't commit," I replied in defiant. "I've already told you it was my ex-boyfriend who did all of this. I stole those pictures so I could blackmail him after he cheated on me. I never killed anybody nor did I ever harm an unborn or live baby." My pleading with this asshole wasn't going anywhere. He didn't believe me. Every time I thought I made a little bit of break through with him and had him on my side, he would revert back to telling me my case was doomed.

"But explaining that to a jury is going to take a lot. Especially because they have pictures of you grabbing a young pregnant girl into your car," he said, raising his eyebrows as if he was looking for an explanation. I think this muthafucka really thought I was guilty.

"I don't even have a car! Isn't it supposed to be innocent until proven guilty?" I screamed. "In this fucking case ya'll bastards are making me guilty until proven innocent!" I put my head down.

"The license plates came back to you," he said calmly. It was as if he hadn't heard anything I had just said. Trying to get anyone to believe me was useless.

I had to shake my head at all the things they had against me and how it had all gone down. Duke had gone so far as to have fake plates put on Brian's car in my name. The police thought they were searching my car and found his newest pictures of me. Everything Duke had planned to do to frame me was working thus far. I also learned he had planted evidence in my house as well—a bloodied t-shirt with blood that matched the DNA of the dead sixteen year old girl.

"I don't' even own a car," I whispered again, still in disbelief. "My ex is doing all of this, planting plates and planting physical evidence. He kidnapped my best friend and now I think she's dead too." I was distraught, tears welling up in my eyes. It must've all sounded like a soap opera to this white, fresh out of law school, little prick.

"I think you should think long and hard before you decide to take this case to trial," the prick repeated himself. I was tired of hearing that same old line. "If you lose, you could be facing life or even worse, the death penalty. Did I also mention they have people willing to testify that you were the mastermind behind the baby snatching and illegal adoption ring?"

I put my head down on the table and just sobbed. There had to be a way for me to get out of this predicament. As it stood now, I was fucked.

"I need to sleep on it. I will get back to you and let you know what I want to do," I said through teary eyes. My attorney stood up and left as if he didn't care either way. The C.O. came and took me to be searched, so I could go back to my cell.

I was really contemplating committing suicide, but they had me in solitary confinement with nothing in my cell that I could even remotely use to kill myself. I was sick of being in solitary confinement, but the jail wasn't trying to take a chance of putting me back in general population after what had happened. I heard all those bitches still wanted a piece of me. They were making threats of death the next time they had the chance to get near me. There was no way I could stay locked up for the rest of my life.

I would rather die first.

CHAPTER 32
DIRTY BITCHES

A few days after I had met with my attorney, the C.O. came to my cell to announce I had a visitor.

That took me off guard because my attorney said he wouldn't be back until it was closer to my next court date. I didn't have but one friend. That was Diamond and she was missing, and I didn't fuck with my family at all. I thought about Diamond almost all day, every day. She was probably lying dead somewhere and would never get a proper burial or memorial. I was alive and it was my fault she was dead.

I got myself together and the C.O. led me to the visit area. You can't imagine my shock when I saw Neeko, the owner of the *Magic City* sitting behind the visitor's table. My heart started racing and my stomach cramped up. I just knew he was there to tell me that they had finally found Diamond dead somewhere. That had to be the only reason Neeko would visit me. I never had a great relationship with him when I worked at the club. I crinkled my eyebrows and slowly walked over to the table where Neeko was sitting, awaiting my arrival. We locked eyes and neither one of us said much at first. I sat down hesitantly and looked at him.

"How you doing Lynise?" Neeko asked, finally taking the initiative to speak up.

"I'm as good as can be expected being locked up in here for something I didn't do," I told him. "What brings you here? You're the last person I expected to see."

"Well, I'm here to tell you some shit I found out. I'm warning you though, it's pretty deep," he said. I felt a strange sense of relief that he didn't say he was there to tell me Diamond was found in the bushes somewhere beat to death or she had suffered some other horrific manner of death.

"See, I know you ain't do all what they saying you did in the news. I know how dirty and low down that nigga, Duke, is," Neeko said.

Finally, somebody who believed me! I thought to myself.

"I'm listening," I replied.

"Lynise, that nigga, Duke, gotta be stopped. He took over my club and pushed me completely out," Neeko told me. "Out on my ass. He just snatched all of my life long hard work right from up under me like a slithering dirty snake." He was raising his voice so I could tell this was a very emotional topic for him.

"How could he do that?" I was very curious to know.

"Easy! That muthafucka called in the IRS on me. When those feds started looking into my shit, they found all types of shit. It was true, I hadn't paid my taxes in a while, but they would've never known. Duke called me out. He was working with those pigs. They put a lien against my club and I could not pay it. That slimy bastard, Duke, came in, paid the lien and back property taxes, and snatched my club from me just like that. Lynise, the *club* is my lifeline and he took it right from under me. He done changed the name of it and everything."

Nothing shocked me anymore, but that didn't change the fact what Duke was doing to me and to Neeko, and had done to Diamond and Brian was a fucking shame.

"What does this has to do with me? He set me up too. He ruined my entire life too, but at least you ain't in jail facing life for two murders you didn't commit or dead like Diamond probably is," I said a little irritated.

"Well, I came here to tell you some more shit. But you have to be ready for this Lynise," Neeko warned me.

"Neeko, nothing can get worse than what I'm going through right now."

"I don't know—" he hesitated.

"Just say what you gotta say," I demanded.

"Diamond is far from dead," he said. It seemed as if his words were coming out of his mouth in slow motion. I leaned across the table and I could feel my heart hammering against the steel edge.

"Your girl, Diamond, was down with this whole thing against you all along," Neeko blurted out.

I had heard people talk about the air leaving their lungs, leaving them grasping for air and speechless. I had never truly experienced it. Until now. When the rest of the words came out of his mouth, it was like he had punched me in the gut. I felt such a pain in my stomach. I could've fallen out of the chair. I had to play it off though.

What is this nightmare I am living?

"What? Get the fuck outta here! I don't believe that shit Neeko!" I snapped back. "Duke kidnapped Diamond, I saw her all bloodied up and tied up in pictures. She is probably somewhere dead and you have the fucking nerve to come here and spread rumors about her!" I had raised my voice so high I was starting to get sideway glances from the correction officers.

"Naw, you got that all wrong," Neeko corrected me. "Diamond and Duke set you up. I'm telling you the truth. I done seen them together! Those pictures were staged. In fact, I hear Diamond was bragging about how good she did the red corn syrup to make it look like blood and how after she took the fake pictures of herself, Duke licked all of the syrup off her naked body and they fucked."

I could've just died right there on the spot hearing this shit.

"Word is, when you told her you was gonna blackmail Duke, she went back and told him right away. See Lynise, the truth of the matter is Diamond was fucking Duke the whole time you was with him. I don't know how you couldn't see that! Duke was supplying Diamond with her drugs and hitting her off with a little money on the side. Even when she called you and told you he was in the club with a bitch the night you came in there and wild out, that was all part of their plan so Duke could start the process of breaking up with you."

My ears were ringing now. With every word, I could feel my blood pressure rising and my insides churning. I was biting down into my cheek so hard I could taste blood in my mouth. Tears were burning at the backs of my eye sockets. No, I hadn't killed anyone. Yes, I could see death in my future. And as much as Neeko's words were getting to me, I didn't want to truly believe it. I couldn't believe it. I didn't have family. I had Diamond. She was all I had. This couldn't be happening.

"I don't believe that shit Neeko," I said, mincing my words. I didn't want to believe my best friend had betrayed me in such a major way.

"I knew you wasn't gon' believe me, so I brought this," Neeko whispered, secretly sliding a picture across to me.

I slid it off the table and turned it over. Needless to say, my jaw dropped open and my eyes went low into evil slits. Sure enough, it was a picture of Diamond and Duke together in the club. Diamond was just fine, sitting on Duke's lap smiling from ear to ear. The thought of her being treated by Duke how I was treated in the beginning threatened to make me throw up or scream. To think whenever Duke did something for me, I would share with her. Meanwhile, she was fucking him and getting shit from him anyway. I couldn't believe my best friend, the bitch I considered my own family, had turned her back on me like this.

I started beating myself up mentally for not going with my first gut that told me Diamond was getting high and not to fuck with her. She would probably have killed her own mama for drugs, so betraying me was nothing to her, I guess. As long as Duke was hitting her off with drugs she was down for whatever.

"I told you I wasn't lying. I ain't got no reason to lie," Neeko said.

"When was this," I croaked out, trying hard to fight back my tears.

"This was a couple of days ago when they were celebrating the fact that Duke took my club from me and is going to hand it over to that bitch Diamond to run it and be part owner in it," Neeko informed me. I didn't trust anybody. Not even Neeko, although he seemed to be there with good intentions . . . and I'm sure, revenge on his mind.

"Why did you come to tell me all of this Neeko? What do you want from me?"

"I came to tell you because unlike ninety-percent of the Tidewater area, I believe that you're innocent," I could hear the anger in his voice. Plus, I like that finally someone believed me. "I also want revenge on the both of them," he continued. "I wanna help you get the fuck out of here and in the end, I know you have a lot of personal information on Duke. I want to destroy this muthafucka, but in the process I want to clean him out. I want him to feel like I feel right now. I don't even know where my next meal is gonna come from. Those fucking IRS assholes froze everything I got."

"But how can I help you? They took everything I had when they raided my apartment," I said somberly.

"Yeah, I know. Diamond told some of my old dancers that are staying loyal to me that she had been planting shit in your room for weeks now. I heard her telling one of the strippers that you were so depressed over Duke that you hadn't even noticed."

I had my fists balled up so tight, it felt like my skin would bust. I didn't want to think about how stupid I had been. My misplaced love for a man who could care less about me probably from the day we met had made me lose my way. He had dogged me with the help of my best friend. I had been played. I deserved better but I had even dogged myself by being head over heels for a lowlife with money and status. I had been something I despised in life—a fool.

"I just need you to give me all of the information about everything Duke has or is into," Neeko continued. "Whatever you know could help me. I am going to follow that muthafucka's every move. I'm going to do some research on every business venture and money-making plan he got going on. I'm going to get the real evidence . . . the evidence that will set you free and put the real criminals behind bars. Once I have them by the fucking throats, I will bring the information to your lawyer to get you freed and the tables will finally turn on Duke. He thinks he is untouchable. But my daddy used to say, 'Dirty is what dirty does.' And Lynise, it's time Duke gets a taste of his own dirty."

I saw something I liked in Neeko's eyes. It was a certain seriousness I had never seen in his eyes before. All of this could only bode well for me. As hard as it was for me to trust anyone, I had to trust Neeko. He may actually be my ticket out of this place.

"Well, I can give you all of the information I have. I had a lot of copies stored in a safety deposit box at the bank. I only have a few of his bank account information in there though and I think I fucked all of those accounts up," I said sadly.

It was a good thing I had made copies of that stuff. I told Neeko what he would need to do in order to get some of the evidence from the box. Then I proceeded to tell Neeko everything I knew about Duke's business dealings from the beginning. If Neeko was going to do me dirty like Duke and Diamond had done, I wouldn't have known it. He seemed to sincerely want to help me. He was my only hope for getting out of jail.

I just hoped he didn't betray me too.

But at this point, what did I have to lose.

Dirty is as dirty does and I wanted that muthafucka, Duke, and that bitch, Diamond, to get just as muddy as me.

Chapter 33
Someway, Somehow

I had waited for days and hadn't heard anything from Neeko.

I had to admit, patience wasn't a virtue for me at the moment. The days were long, the time dragged slowly. I knew lonely and lonely knew me. We weren't the best of friends, but we had to tolerate each other. Actually, I had to tolerate the loneliness. But it made me feel good thinking loneliness had to tolerate me as well.

Depression was my real enemy and that was an understatement. I played out so many scenarios in my mind. In the first and frequently recurring scenario I believed Neeko was working for Duke and Diamond all along and he took the stuff I had in the safety deposit box and handed it all over to Duke. I cursed my lawyer for not agreeing to go get it in the first place. It was the scenario I couldn't get out of my head. Trust was an issue but being incarcerated is a real thing and definitely makes the mind haywire. But I still believed in a hope and a prayer . . . I didn't have a choice. I needed to be-lieve in something.

On this day, I was being let out of my cell for my one-hour recreation. This time I asked the C.O. if I could get the newspaper or get library books. The C.O. was kind enough to give me the newspaper if I agreed to just stay in my bunk. She obviously didn't feel like standing outside watching me do nothing for an hour. I agreed. I sat down on my hard ass bunk and opened the first page of the newspaper.

"No! No! No! Oh God!" I screamed when I saw the top news headline. There was a large picture of Neeko splashed on the first page and the caption:

Former Magic City Club Owner Found Murdered Ex-ecution Style

All the hope I had of getting out of jail was dashed away. I doubled over with stomach pains. I couldn't even read the story because I already knew what had probably happened to Neeko. I also knew what had probably happened to all of my information that I had kept for safe keepings.

In the days following Neeko's news, I didn't eat and I barely slept. I had settled on the fact I would just take the plea deal and do time for something I didn't do. When my lawyer finally came to visit me, I was prepared to tell him just that. He was looking surprisingly excited and I wasn't in the fucking mood for him.

"Lynise! I have something to tell you," my lawyer said as I sat down. He had never referred to me by my first name.

I stretched my sore, red-rimmed eyes to look at him. I was going to listen to him again before I told him I would take the plea deal.

"We have an emergency hearing tomorrow to ask the judge to dismiss the case against you!" my lawyer sang out.

"What?" I asked, very confused. Definitely more confused than excited. Doing time did that to you.

"Somebody dropped a package off at my office with a bunch of mitigating evidence that puts holes in the prosecution's case. Most of it points the finger at some very important city officials," he said.

"Neeko! Oh my God! He risked his life!" I shouted out through tears of joy.

My lawyer looked at me strangely. He didn't ask me for any explanations but he told me not to tell anyone in the jail about the new developments in my case.

Hell, who could I tell . . . I was in solitary confinement and *didn't have a friend in the world?*

It was two days before we could get an emergency hearing. I didn't sleep a total of three hours in those two days. When I appeared in a very secretive closed court session, my lawyer asked for an immediate dismissal of the case. The judge said she needed a few hours to review the new evidence and make a decision. I sat in the courthouse holding cell on the edge of my seat.

"Ms. Washington, it's time to go back to court," a courtroom deputy called out to me. I stood up on wobbly legs and let him cuff me and lead me into the courtroom. When I looked over at my lawyer I couldn't tell anything from his facial expression. He had on a serious poker face. I gulped down a lump of fear.

I stood behind the defense table and the judge looked over at me. I was wringing my hands in front of me, a sign of pure nerves.

"Ms. Washington, after reviewing the newly received evidence and new development in this case," the judge began. "And after a review of the evidence compiled against you, and the fact that that evidence may have been acquired on a warrant obtained without full probable cause, it is this court's position that the state's case against you for the murder of Tania Blackmon, Brian Curtis and the list of crimes associated with the illegal adoption and sale of several unidentified babies, is dismissed without prejudice."

I fell backwards into the hard wooden chair. I was very weak and couldn't believe it. I grabbed a hold of my lawyer and just started balling. The judge banged her gavel.

"I am not finished counselor and Ms. Washington," the judge admonished. My lawyer urged me to stand back up. "With this case being dismissed without prejudice, this arrest will be expunged from your client's records. However, in light of the seriousness of this case, your client is expected to make herself available to assist the prosecution in their case to find the real killer or killers, and baby snatcher. Should your client refuse to cooperate, she could be held in contempt of this court, as it is my direct order for her to keep herself available. Is this understood?"

"Yes, your honor! Yes, I will do whatever it takes," I cried out.

"Good. Now go get on with your life and let's work together to get whoever committed all of these crimes," she said, cracking a little smile.

I was in total agreement. I knew just where to look and just how to do that too.

Duke Carrington had not seen the last of me.

Epilogue

The judge told me to make myself available to the cops and assist in finding the killer and baby snatcher.

Hell, I knew the killer and baby snatcher. Probably half the Virginia Beach Police Department also knew Duke Carrington was the criminal mastermind behind the killings and baby snatching ring. So my thought as I was being released was, *Why should I help people who already know the criminal responsible for the crimes.*

So why in the hell should I stay in Virginia Beach? It was a valid thought. Yes, I wanted my revenge against both Duke and Diamond, but who in the hell was I and how could I pull this off by myself. Plus, I had to be realistic. My thirst for vengeance was why I had spent time in the joint for shit I didn't do. My original plan of turning that muthafucka in was the plan I should have stuck with. And walking out of this place I couldn't believe I still had this shit on my mind. I was certifiably crazy. I knew it. I had to be beyond stupid to want to go after Duke or even consider going after him and Diamond.

And Diamond, that bitch! I could see and feel myself kicking that bitch's ass. I know she would be surprised to see me. She would be even more surprise when I just walked up to her ass and cold punch that bitch in her face. I would repeatedly attack her face with my fists. She would think I was Muhammad Ali on her ass. And once I knocked that slut down, I would kick her entire body from head to toe.

As much I knew I should just drop this shit, in my mind, I couldn't. I needed some kind of vengeance . . . even if it was just kicking Diamond's ass and suffering the wrath of Duke.

That bitch owed me.

The more I thought about the hell I went through being an inmate for the short time I was in jail, the more I realized I was lucky as hell to walk out of this hellhole. And this was jail. Prison would have ruined me. I got my ass kicked, my face fucked up, my cheek wired up because jailhouse hoes thought I killed young girls and stole babies. My reputation wasn't shit now. *And why?* Because the one person I believed in, the one person I loved as family, the only family I thought I had said fuck me. Probably jealous over some petty shit like I once had Duke doing for me or choosing me over her worthless, slimy ass.

As I walked down the long sidewalk of the Virginia Beach Jail for Women, I was surprised to see a black stretch Hummer. The windows of it had been tinted and the rims of it looked really expensive. I wondered who the truck was there to pick up. I looked behind me and didn't see anyone. *Whoever it is, she is a lucky bitch,* I thought.

My mind was on catching a bus and possibly calling someone to loan me enough money for a motel room for a few nights.

When I got to the end of the sidewalk, the back door opened and a female got out. I knew her, knew her well. Her name was Kat, short for Katrina. She was Neeko's main girl. They had two daughters together. The rumor was she was Neeko's first dancer at the *Magic City*. He immediately had a thing for her. She stopped dancing and became Neeko's manager. She managed the money, took care of the business end of their enterprise. And the most important part I remembered about her was she was a scary bitch.

"Get in," she commanded me. I was afraid, actually very leery to get in the car with Neeko's widow. Even though they weren't legally married, I was sure she thought of Neeko's death as losing a husband.

"Did you hear me?" she said. Her voice was cold and hard. My feet were stuck in cement. I couldn't move.

When the oversize driver got out of the truck, I decided to cooperate.

I slid in and she came in after me, closing the door behind her. The truck immediately pulled off. I sat with my back to the driver in the big truck. Sitting across from me was Kat and next to her was one of the finest men I had ever seen. Also, someone I had seen on several occasions at the *Magic City.*

"You remember, Ms. Washington," Mr. Tall and Sexy asked me. He stood at least six feet three, slender and fit. His hair was chopped short and what shadow of hair he had was visibly wavy. Combined with his neatly cut mustache that connected to his chin and facial hair made him someone I wish was in my bed every night.

"Yes sir. They call you The Bishop," I replied. He was the kingpin. The master criminal that ran things from D.C. to the Big Apple . . . from selling drugs to running illegal upscale gambling establishments to money laundering, The Bishop was the man. He had visited the club on several occasions and he and Neeko were very friendly with each other.

He smiled and slightly laughed. "Ms. Washington, my name is Buckley Bishop," he said in a proper voice with perfect diction. "Neeko was my older brother."

My mouth dropped open. This was the last thing I would have thought. Why didn't Neeko tell anyone? Why did he even sweat the shit Duke did to him? He could have called his brother, The Bishop.

"What you want from me?" I asked timidly.

"Any and everything you can tell us about Duke Carrington and his operation," Kat answered with attitude. She was now sporting dark sunglasses. I knew she was still hurting. I understood . . . especially if she knew Neeko was trying to help me.

"Ms. Washington, Neeko and I have different fathers," The Bishop volunteered. "But it didn't stop him from being there for me when our father died. My mother was a junkie and our father died when I was eight. Neeko was nineteen then, the oldest of my dad's five kids. He literally worked two jobs and got his hustle on to take care of the four of us. Three of the four of us went to college, thanks to Neeko."

The Bishop stopped. He was staring in my eyes. It was a steady stare. No sadness. His eyes were soft, but very serious.

"Bottom line, Ms. Washington," he began again. "I want Duke Carrington . . . and I want you to tell me everything you know about him and his operation. And by everything, I mean everything. If his favorite color is black, tell me that, if he licks his own balls, I want to know that too.

"Neeko never asked me for anything. As you know, he would even let me and my entourage come to his club and let us have the run of the place without us spending a penny. Why? Because he was still being the big brother.

"So believe me when I tell you this . . . Mr. Carrington will hate the day he ever heard of Lynise Aaliyah Washington. He will finally understand what Johnnie Taylor meant by, *it's cheaper to keep her.*"

I finally smiled. He was right! I looked at Kat, then at Mr. Buckley Bishop, aka The Bishop. I had my team. I was ripe for my revenge. The Bishop reached his hand out and I shook it. This was followed by Kat doing the same thing.

Duke, it would've been cheaper to keep me, bitch, I thought as I sat back and enjoyed the ride.

COMING SOON

KIKI SWINSON
PRESENTS

Cheaper to Keep Her
PART 2 THE SAGA CONTINUES

2

A NOVEL
UNIQUE

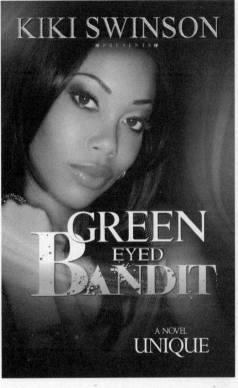

KIKI SWINSON
PRESENTS

GREEN EYED BANDIT

A NOVEL
UNIQUE